THE
MEASURE
OF A MAN

MAGGIE LEE

D1714026

Dreamspinner Press

Published by
Dreamspinner Press
5032 Capital Circle SW
Ste 2, PMB# 279
Tallahassee, FL 32305-7886
USA
http://www.dreamspinnerpress.com/

The Measure of a Man
Copyright © 2012 by Maggie Lee

Cover Art by Reese Dante
http://www.reesedante.com

ISBN: 978-1-62380-250-9

Printed in the United States of America
First Edition
December 2012

eBook edition available
eBook ISBN: 978-1-62380-251-6

CHAPTER 1

ALEC WESTON opened his eyes with a start; every muscle tensed as he tried to pinpoint exactly what had woken him from sleep. Not that he slept very soundly these days, what with the knowledge that he and his two companions were being pursued by the City Guard and the Sun League—two different foes, each intent on its own unique brand of retribution.

While his eyes grew accustomed to the dark, he listened to the noises all around him, attuned to anything that might signal danger. The slow, even breathing coming from the warm body tucked up against his side indicated that Kit Porter, his former captive, was still fast asleep. The more guttural sounds emanating from the floor beside the narrow cot told him that Robert Warren, his best friend and former second-in-command, was also dozing. Alec strained his ears, casting beyond the wooden walls of the shabby tavern room, hearing nothing more alarming than the potboy dragging firewood across the kitchen floor. A moment later he heard the sound of a slap and a muffled sob, followed by a sharply hissed order. The unfortunate lad had obviously started the day on the wrong side of the innkeeper, although Alec wasn't sure that the sullen, pinch-faced Elijah Oates had anything but wrong sides.

Rolling over carefully, Alec hitched up onto his side and glanced around. The first pale rays of sunlight were stealing through the cracks in the splintered shutter and inching across the room, illuminating the depressing scene. The tiny space had once been a storeroom and was still heaped high with ironbound kegs and burlap grain sacks. Some foodstuffs had been hastily removed, but the acrid smell of rotting vegetables still hung heavy in the air. A single bed was jammed up against one wall, with a thin, straw-filled pallet tossed onto the dirt floor beside it. Oates had made it clear that their few coins warranted nothing more than the most basic necessities, though he acted as if he was doing them the greatest of favors by allowing them lodgings.

From the calculating look he had given them when they'd washed up here two days ago, Alec suspected that he knew they were on the run, although clearly he hadn't guessed from whom. If he'd known that both the Lord Chancellor's City Guard and the outlawed Sun League were hunting Alec and his small party, he would have surely turned them in to one or the other. As it was, he'd quickly pocketed their money and shown them to this wretched hole, turfing the potboy out and into the scullery to fend off the rats and the damp while Alec, Kit, and Robert made the best of their miserable situation.

The sounds from the adjacent kitchen grew louder as preparations for the day got underway. Alec knew that they were wearing out what little welcome had been extended; they would have to leave before Oates's curiosity overcame his immediate avarice and he decided to find out who they were and how he could profit further from them. Besides, Alec knew it was dangerous to stay in one place for too long; although the Lord Chancellor's men were unlikely to come digging around the barren backwaters of Cardeston, the Sun League would soon have its spies rooting around the area.

Beside him, Kit stirred, and Alec reached to smooth a hand through the younger man's tangled hair until he settled again with a deep sigh. Kit Porter—the reason he and Robert had abandoned their home, their reputation, and their position in the City Guard and were now hunted men. A week ago they had arrested Kit on the orders of Anthony Arlen, the Lord Chancellor, and were escorting him to trial at the county court of Shrewsbury. Alec had been uneasy from the start, sensing that things were not as they appeared. It had taken a little while to tease out the truth, but Alec had gradually come to realize that Kit was not a common pickpocket, as he had been led to believe, but was the intimate companion of Marcus de Crecy, an influential leader of the Sun League, whose network of thieves and cutthroats seemed to operate with impunity in the northern shires. Arlen had planned to force Kit to give evidence against de Crecy, and had threatened him with death if he refused to cooperate. What Arlen had not foreseen was that Kit would choose the noose rather than betray the League and put the lives of his family in danger. Alec and Robert had ended up with two terrible options: follow orders and deliver Kit to his death, or risk their lives and their future by setting him free.

"Everything alright, Alec?" Robert's whispered question interrupted Alec's idle musing.

"Aye," he murmured. "Everything's fine."

Robert sat up, rubbing at his bleary eyes. "You're thinking it's time to move on." It wasn't a question, and Alec smiled at his friend's certainty.

"Aye," he repeated. "Oates is asking too many questions. It's only a matter of time before he starts digging further afield."

Robert nodded. "He'd sell us out as soon as look at us."

Alec shrugged. "Can you really blame him?" he asked ruefully. "Between Arlen and the Sun League, I don't know which I'd fear the most. Either one would destroy him if they knew he was harboring us."

Robert snorted. "Either one would pay him a pretty penny if he handed us over, you mean."

"It amounts to the same thing," Alec replied. "We need to move on."

Robert yawned and stretched, grimacing as he worked the stiffness out of his muscles. Alec had taken a turn tossing sleeplessly on the thin pallet, and he winced in sympathy. For him, it had been an easy choice to help Kit evade Arlen's sinister plotting and escape the cruel abuse he had received at the hands of Marcus de Crecy. Alec's growing attraction to the beautiful young man had played a significant part in his decision. But Alec suspected that Robert was here as much from a steadfast loyalty to his captain as from his own outraged sense of justice; he hoped that Robert would never have cause to regret his allegiance.

"I can't say I'll miss the accommodations," Robert muttered.

Alec suppressed a sigh, trying not to think about the comfortable house he had forsaken, with its soft feather bed and large cedar chest filled with clean clothes. He absently scratched the fresh fleabites that reddened his forearm, his nose wrinkling in distaste at the smell of the unwashed clothing he'd worn, day and night, since they'd given Arlen's men the slip in Shrewsbury and taken to the road. That had been four days ago; two spent thundering their mounts through the heavily wooded shire, putting as much distance as they could between Arlen and themselves, and two spent holed up in this miserable rat trap trying to avoid the Sun League's roaming agents.

Kit moaned in his sleep and shuffled restlessly; Alec glanced down and once more tried to soothe him back to sleep. They were all exhausted, but the emotional toll of the past few days had combined with the hurts Kit had received in a recent fall. Though he was the youngest of them, Kit seemed most affected by their current ordeal. He settled under Alec's stroking hand, sighing as his body relaxed against the straw-filled ticking. Kit was lying on his stomach, and Alec gently traced his fingers over the ugly raised scars that crisscrossed his back, anger rising at the thought of the man who had put them there.

"That bastard will never touch him again," Robert promised softly.

Alec looked up into concerned brown eyes and was grateful for Robert's assurances, however tenuous they might be. Kit had spent three years in servitude to Marcus de Crecy and would always bear the man's scars. Some years ago, Alec had suffered similarly at the hands of the Sun League, and his own welted body was a mirror image to Kit's. He sometimes wondered if it was why he felt such a deep connection to the young man, despite only knowing him for a short span of time.

"Do you think de Crecy is hunting Kit himself?" Alec asked.

Robert's face darkened. "If he is, he'll have cause to regret it when I get my hands on him."

"You'll have to stand in line, my friend," Alec countered. An arrow de Crecy had loosed at Kit when they first took flight had missed its mark and lodged in Alec's shoulder instead; he took grim satisfaction in plotting his revenge on the man, the reasons steadily mounting as they discovered more awful truths about him from Kit.

"It's impossible to sleep with you two gabbing like a pair of fishwives!"

Alec stilled his hand at Kit's grumbling voice, and he withdrew it quickly as the young man rolled onto his back and smiled up at him, his eyes brimming with affection. Alec eased away from Kit's body as sudden arousal coursed through him. Although they had admitted their attraction to each other, there had been little time or opportunity to explore it further, and Alec felt an unaccustomed awkwardness about the hardness stirring between his legs.

Robert climbed slowly to his feet. "I'll go rustle up some breakfast," he mumbled.

Alec smiled at his departing back. Neither he nor Kit had spoken to Robert about the feelings that had grown between them, but Robert seemed to instinctively know, far too shrewd to have missed the signs that Alec had scarcely been aware of himself. When Robert left, closing the door behind him, Alec turned his smile on Kit.

"Sleep well?" he asked.

Kit grimaced. "I might as well be sleeping on the floor for all the comfort this bed offers."

"It will likely get worse before it gets better," Alec said apologetically. There was no point prevaricating; they all knew that the road ahead was going to be difficult.

"Have you decided where we're going?" Kit asked, and Alec couldn't fail to detect the wistful anticipation in his voice.

Alec had known where they were heading from the minute they'd fled Shrewsbury; he suspected Robert knew it too, though they hadn't yet spoken of it. It was becoming increasingly obvious that they would have to leave the shire, and for that they would need help. But evading both Arlen's soldiers and the Sun League's far-reaching web of supporters was going to be a challenge. He'd spent the last few days checking routes and gathering information while trying not to draw too much attention to himself; he was hopeful that today he could finalize the details of their escape.

"I'll be sure by the end of the day," he promised.

Kit nodded, seemingly satisfied. He stretched his arms above his head, his lean body brushing against Alec's side, making his prick twitch and fill further. Alec tried not to groan as warm, supple flesh slid against him, heating his own skin. He looked down into Kit's flushed face, eyes heavy-lidded with sleep, soft lips wind-chapped and slightly parted, and he leaned in and placed a gentle kiss on the upturned mouth. Kit reached out and pulled him close, and they clung together for a moment while Alec's erection throbbed rhythmically between them. He pulled back, his senses reeling, afraid that he'd push beyond the point of control. Kit moaned aloud at the sudden separation, but there was something close to relief in his eyes.

"Better get a move on," Alec said gruffly. "Another long day ahead of us."

Kit murmured his assent and swung his legs onto the floor. Alec was oddly gratified to see the gentle swell that tented Kit's cotton drawers, reassured that his own desire was echoed in the younger man, even as Kit seemed unsure how to act on the feelings. Alec couldn't blame him, schooled as he had been to service Marcus de Crecy's perverse appetites, with no expectation of receiving pleasure himself.

Kit crossed the few steps to the doorway and fished his shirt off the floor; he pulled it on and tucked it tightly into the top of his breeches. When they were alone, he no longer concealed the sunburst tattoo that had been carved into his flesh when he'd been abducted by the League, but he was careful to hide it from other prying eyes, knowing how rapidly word would spread if it were spotted. Alec watched as he combed his fingers through the long strands of his chestnut hair, trying to tease out the tangles. Eventually giving up with a sigh, Kit swiftly braided his hair as best he could and looked up expectantly.

"Go find Robert," Alec said. "I'll be right out."

Kit turned obediently and left the room, and Alec dropped back onto the mattress with a frustrated sigh, though it only took a brief moment of considering their situation for his erection to deflate.

Given that their resources were drying up quickly, Alec knew that the sooner they completed the next leg of their journey, the better. Getting out of the shire was their first priority. Alec suspected that the Lord Chancellor's men would be less likely to pursue them once they'd left the county. Anthony Arlen's pride might be wounded at letting Kit slip through his fingers, but he was too pragmatic a man to waste resources on a lost cause.

Marcus de Crecy was a different proposition altogether. From what Alec had seen of the man's behavior, and from the stories Kit had gradually shared, de Crecy appeared to be willing to go to any lengths to get back what he considered his. In addition, the Sun League's power and influence extended way beyond the borders of the tiny shire of Salop, its malevolent tentacles stretching from coast to coast. Alec wasn't sure how far they would have to travel to outrun the League, which did not give up its members easily, no matter how unwillingly they had joined.

Shaking his head, Alec rolled off the lumpy mattress and prepared to join his companions, wondering fleetingly how much each suspected about the direness of their situation.

THE sun was barely skimming the horizon when Kit stumbled out of the inn, spotting Robert seated at a rough wooden table in the forecourt. Although chilly in the early hours, they preferred to break fast outside rather than risk the speculative looks of the diverse groups of travelers passing through the inn each day.

Robert mumbled a greeting when Kit slid onto the bench opposite him. His mouth was full of the coarse dark bread that was all the innkeeper provided for them in the morning. Kit pulled off a hunk, its texture and moldy taste indicating that it was at least a few days old. He ate it anyway, preferring the stale fare to an empty stomach.

"I'll be damned glad when we put this dismal place behind us," Robert muttered.

"Do you think we'll leave soon?" Kit asked.

Robert shrugged. "As soon as the captain gives the order," he replied.

Kit bit into a piece of bread, hiding a smile. Robert had spent several years as second-in-command to Alec, and he seemed to be having a hard time remembering that Alec was no longer a captain in the City Guard. Kit guessed that old habits would be hard to break.

He looked up when Alec walked out of the inn and stopped by the table long enough to grab up the last piece of bread.

"On your way out?" Robert asked.

Alec nodded. "One last foray. We'll leave at first light tomorrow."

Kit was glad to hear it; he was beginning to hate this place with its watchful, surly innkeeper and dank lodgings, and he found the endless hours of restless waiting almost unendurable. Whatever dangers and privations they might face on the open road were infinitely preferable to this half life. He rose as Alec walked off, followed him to the stable, and watched as he saddled his horse.

"I don't suppose you'd let me come with you?" he asked hopefully.

As expected, Alec shook his head. "You're safer here with Robert," he replied, avoiding eye contact.

Kit sighed heavily, but didn't argue. Robert had stuck closer to him than his own shadow, and Kit suspected that Alec had ordered him not to let Kit out of his sight. The constant surveillance was too reminiscent of life with the Sun League, and it was starting to chafe.

"We'll be on our way tomorrow, I promise," Alec said. "I want to check one more route, but come what may, we're leaving."

Kit was grateful and hoped it showed. Alec tugged at his cinch one last time, then grabbed up his reins and walked his mount into the cobbled courtyard before boosting up into the saddle.

"Don't get into any mischief," he said, smiling down at Kit.

Kit's mouth twitched into a grin. "I was just about to say the same thing," he said. He reached and covered Alec's knee with his hand. "Don't stay out too long," he said anxiously, then, afraid that his apprehension would distract Alec, he added, "Robert's role of mother hen is wearing thin."

Alec laughed and edged away from Kit's hand before trotting off with a parting wave.

Kit watched until he disappeared, then turned reluctantly and walked back to the table. Robert had finished eating and was now carefully oiling his sword and polishing it to a high sheen. Kit resumed his seat, there being little else to do until Alec returned.

Robert's hands moved confidently over the sword, taking care to wipe every inch. Sunlight glinted off the burnished blade, the tiny nicks along its sharp edge a testament to its frequent use. Robert's face was a mask of concentration, and Kit suddenly noticed the deepening of the small wrinkles at the corner of his friend's mouth, and the dark circles under his eyes that stood out in contrast to the pallor of his skin. He hadn't trimmed his beard for days, and small flecks of gray were becoming increasingly noticeable. He seemed to have aged in just a short time, and Kit felt a sharp stab of remorse that he had dragged this man from his comfortable life and entangled him in a business not his own.

"We could do something about that, you know."

Kit looked about in confusion. Robert nodded toward his hands, and Kit realized he'd been unconsciously fiddling with his braid, trying to tug the knotted mess into some semblance of order.

Marcus had never let him so much as trim his hair into shape, preferring the long, shining mane that wrapped around Kit like a cloak. Kit had to admit that he'd grown vain about his thick locks, although that was in the days when he'd had the time and resources to keep his hair neat and clean. Since they had taken to the road, it had become increasingly more tangled and unmanageable.

"I suppose we could cut it all off," Kit said, warming to the idea as soon as the words were spoken.

"I'm not sure Alec will approve," Robert said doubtfully.

Kit grinned. "We'd better get it done before he gets back, then," he said. "Besides, it will help disguise me."

Robert frowned, but in the end, he shrugged. "It's your decision," he said.

Kit felt a jolt of shock at the simplicity of that statement. For three years, everything in his world had been dictated by Marcus de Crecy; his every word, every action, and in the end almost every thought had been shaped and determined for him. That he now had control over his own life, even if it were only in this small thing, was almost too much to take in.

"Let's do it," he declared.

He only tensed once, when Robert withdrew his hunting knife from its leather scabbard and wrapped Kit's long braid around his fingers.

"You're sure?" Robert asked, the blade hovering just beside Kit's ear.

"I'm sure," Kit said with certainty. He felt a sharp tug at his scalp as Robert used his knife to saw through the strands of hair, and a moment later Robert's hand appeared in front of his face, the long chestnut braid hanging limply from his fist. Kit felt a single moment of regret, then a flash of buoyancy overtook him, and he shook his head, laughing out loud.

"Hold still while I tidy you up," Robert growled. He continued hacking for a few minutes more, then stepped around Kit and looked at him critically. "You'll do," he said, wiping the knife on his jerkin before sheathing it.

Kit ran his hand through his shorn locks, relishing the unfamiliar weightlessness. It wasn't close-cropped, like Robert's, it still brushed the high collar of his shirt, but the joy he felt had little to do with the actual length, and everything to do with the freedom to make his own choice.

He almost regretted his decision when he saw the shocked look on Alec's face as he rode back into the courtyard some hours later. Kit noticed that Robert, who had been stuck to his side all morning, suddenly disappeared when Alec thundered in.

"What on earth happened to you?" Alec demanded, his eyes widening as he slid off his horse and got a good look.

"It was a mess," Kit said defensively, busying himself with Alec's horse. He felt the man's eyes on him, even when he turned his back, and he knew that the hot flush that stained his cheeks was also burning his neck bright red. A long moment later, he felt Alec's hand comb through his shortened hair.

"I like it," Alec declared, as relief flooded Kit. "It makes you look older."

Kit turned and smiled into Alec's amused eyes as Alec reached to tuck a strand behind Kit's ear.

"Beautiful," he murmured. He traced a line with his finger across Kit's cheekbone, and Kit wasn't sure whether the heat he felt coursing through his body was emanating from the steaming coat of Alec's snorting horse or from some deep well inside himself.

"Did you have any luck?" he asked, cursing silently when Alec shook himself and dropped his hand.

"Aye, I did," Alec replied abruptly. "Where's Robert? We need to make plans."

SUPPER was a dismal affair, only palatable because Kit knew that this was the last meal they would endure in this squalid place. Bad weather had forced them into the inn's small dining room, where they huddled at a table close to the fireplace, trying to extract what little warmth they could from the barely glowing embers in the grate. Elijah Oates's miserliness seemed to know no bounds, and despite the wind whistling down the chimney and through the cracks in the wooden walls, he refused to allow the fire to be banked higher.

There were only two other occupied tables when Kit and his friends made their way into the room, and the men seated at them kept their heads bent over their food, seemingly indifferent to new arrivals. It suited Kit very well, and he knew Alec and Robert felt the same.

Too stingy to employ a serving girl, Oates was tending the tables himself, with the help of Ned, the poor lad who was as much whipping boy as potboy. Kit smiled when Ned approached their table carrying a wooden tray on which balanced three bowls of watery soup.

"You'll be able to have your bed back tomorrow," Kit said kindly.

Ned raised startled eyes. The lad was a mute, and it was likely that most people overlooked him; he certainly seemed unused to being spoken to directly. He nodded a fraction, his gaze darting furtively toward Oates.

"I suspect it's a mite warmer than the scullery," Kit continued.

Ned nodded again before scurrying back to the kitchen, shoulders hunched as he passed Oates, as though expecting a blow.

"He's scared stiff," Kit said, casting a dark look in Oates's direction.

"He's probably some local orphan glad of a dry bed and a daily crust," Robert said.

"It isn't any kind of life—" Kit started.

"There are worse situations to be in," Robert interrupted sharply.

Kit held his tongue and concentrated on the thin soup in front of him. He hardly needed a lecture on the inequities and hardships of life, but he was too weary to quarrel with Robert.

"I want to leave at dawn," Alec said quickly, clearly trying to avert an argument. "We'll travel southeast. We're going to shadow the main road and make our way to Ludlow. Then we'll head for the county border."

Robert arched an eyebrow. "If we traveled directly eastward, we'd be out of the shire in half the time," he said.

"Which is exactly what everybody will expect," Alec said reasonably. "They'll presume we'll make for the border as quickly as possible, and they'll be lying in wait for us."

"So instead we're going to travel to the most populated town in the county, outside of Shrewsbury," Robert observed dryly.

"We have a better chance of staying out of sight in a large town than in any of the smaller villages," Alec pointed out.

Kit felt his gut tighten as the conversation progressed; neither Alec nor Robert stopped to ask his opinion on the matter as they hammered out the details of the journey that was destined to change their lives irrevocably. His gaze shifted between the two of them, watching wordlessly as they exchanged ideas, until finally there was a pause in the conversation.

"If we're traveling to Ludlow, we'll have to ride directly past Church Stretton," he said. "I can't leave the shire until I see my mother."

He flinched as Robert rounded on him, a frown on his face. "Out of the question," Robert said firmly. "The League will be expecting that. Doubtless they stationed men at your mother's house the moment you disappeared."

"Then we'll have to find some way through," Kit said.

"Kit, it's too dangerous," Alec put in. His eyes were filled with sympathy, though the rest of his features hardened into determined resistance.

"I won't go without seeing her," Kit repeated doggedly, afraid to hear his voice crack, though his resolve was unwavering.

"That's ridiculous," Robert hissed. "I've risked enough already. I'll not put my life on the line because you can't sever your mother's apron strings—"

"I have to know she will not suffer because of my actions," Kit cut in. "Until I know she and my sisters are safe, I cannot continue this journey. I'll not trade their lives for my freedom."

He clamped his lips together as Ned sidled up to the table and deposited three plates slopping over with a congealed mess of vegetables and stringy beef. While the young boy cleared away their empty soup bowls, Kit found the courage to glance up at his companions. Robert was scowling fiercely, his face bright red with anger; Alec was watching him intently, his deep blue eyes sharp and focused, as though he was looking at something beyond Kit's flushed face. Kit bit his lip, his eyes pleading silently for understanding, and as Ned backed away from the table, Alec's features softened.

"We'll make the stop," he said quietly.

"Alec, it's madness," Robert protested.

Alec raised a hand, cutting off the impending diatribe. "I'll understand if you can't support this plan," he said, turning to face his old friend. "But it's something Kit has to do. We could meet up further along the road if you wish it."

Robert looked incredulously between them, as though they had both lost their wits. Then he shook his head. "You're fools. Both of you," he said tersely. "But we're in this together, come what may."

Kit felt a rush of gratitude. "Thank you," he stammered.

"I hope we don't end up regretting this foolish decision," Robert muttered darkly, unhappiness coming off him in waves. "I have no intention of ending my days skewered on the business end of a Sun League sword!"

They finished the rest of their meal in strained silence and retired early. Kit offered to take his turn sleeping on the pallet on the floor, but Robert waved him off impatiently and rolled himself up in his cloak, and moments later his soft snores echoed around the darkened room.

Kit turned onto his side to face Alec, picking out his strong features in the glow of moonlight filtering through the shutters. "Thank you," he whispered. "I know you don't like to disagree with Robert."

"Especially when he's right," Alec observed wryly. "You understand how dangerous this will be?"

Kit breathed in deeply, getting his roiling stomach under control. "I understand. If you'd prefer not to accompany me—" He yelped in surprise as Alec cuffed him lightly on the ear.

"Like Robert said, we're in this together."

"I'm indebted to him... to you both," Kit murmured. He'd said the same words over and again since Alec and Robert had set him free instead of turning him over to the Lord Chancellor, though he never felt they truly understood how deeply grateful he was.

"Underneath that tough hide, Robert is a very good man," Alec said.

Kit didn't need the reminder; Robert had proven to be loyal, forthright, and above all, just. Although his gruffness still scared Kit a little, he had come to deeply respect Robert's integrity.

"As are you," he said fervently.

Alec's teeth flashed in a smile, and he reached to cup Kit's cheek. "I have other motives," he whispered.

Kit turned his head and kissed the warm palm, hardened by years gripping the handle of a sword. "I'm glad of it," he said. He felt a familiar twitch in his groin as his cock lengthened and filled. He'd felt this attraction from the moment he'd looked up into Captain Alec

Weston's vivid blue eyes and strong, handsome face, and the feeling had only intensified as he discovered what kind of man Alec was: kind, fair, and honest right to his core. Despite three years sharing Marcus de Crecy's bed, Kit had never experienced the kind of desire that stirred when Alec Weston was near him, though he felt oddly shy about turning that yearning into action. With Marcus, things had been simple, the man only too eager to teach Kit how to please him, and quick to lash out if he didn't learn swiftly enough. But Alec was decent and honorable, and Kit didn't know whether he had anything to offer a man like that.

Alec leaned in and brushed his lips against Kit's, but he pulled back before things could get more heated, leaving Kit feeling both abandoned and, conversely, relieved. "You need to get some sleep," Alec whispered. "We have a long road ahead of us."

Kit turned onto his side and settled against Alec's broad chest, content to feel Alec's arm snake around his waist and hold him close. He wasn't sure that he'd be able to fall asleep, aroused as he was by Alec's presence, but the soft sound of Robert's steady breathing soon lulled him, and he drifted off, feeling happy and secure.

WHEN Alec woke this time, he knew instantly what had disturbed his rest—the sound of horses' hooves, as recognizable as his own heartbeat. He cocked his head and listened intently, judging that three riders had just entered the courtyard, taking absolutely no pains to muffle their noise even though it was barely daybreak. The newcomers must have woken Oates, because a moment later Alec heard him holler for Ned, then the shuffle of feet as the two of them hurried to the door, which was being violently rapped upon. Alec was instantly wide awake, wondering who was arrogant enough to disregard the conventions of decency, knowing at least two parties for whom propriety held little sway: the City Guard and the Sun League.

He heard Oates, in his most unctuous tone, welcoming the "gentlemen" to his humble inn, followed by the heavy footfalls of three men, and the noisy clatter as baggage was tossed onto the stone floor. Alec tensed as the party passed the door to the storage room, but calmed as they continued on their way, clearly being shown to their rooms. Silence fell once more, and Alec was just beginning to relax when the door to the room creaked, then inched open slowly to allow a shadowy figure to slip inside.

Alec had scarcely registered the intruder before Robert sprang to his feet, and in one swift motion pinned the slight body against the wooden wall, his dagger pressed dangerously against the figure's exposed throat.

A strangled sound, urgent and guttural, alerted Alec to the identity of the boy trembling under his friend's glinting blade. "Robert," he barked, but even as he spoke, Robert was withdrawing the knife.

"What are you about?" Robert growled.

Ned flinched, his eyes darting frantically between Robert's towering body and the bed. Kit shot up, finally disturbed enough to be dragged out of his deep sleep. He glanced around, swiveling his head rapidly from Alec to Robert, before his gaze fixed on Ned's quivering form. When he registered the identity of the boy, he swung his legs out of bed and swiftly crossed the room before shouldering Robert aside.

"Ned, it's alright," he said, his voice gentle, as though crooning to a wounded animal. He cradled Ned's cheek, the gesture soothing the boy's violent shivering. "What is it?" Kit asked.

Ned waved his hand, pointing to the door and grunting. Kit looked confused, and Alec slid out of bed and crossed the floor to come up behind him.

"The men who just arrived?" he hazarded.

The boy's head nodded madly.

"What of them, son?" Robert's voice was deliberately gentle, but Ned stiffened nonetheless. Alec gestured briefly, and Robert took a few steps back. Ned relaxed visibly and turned back to face Kit. He pointed again to the door, his unintelligible sounds growing more frantic. Kit looked around, his taut features revealing his frustration at not understanding the struggling young boy.

"You want to tell us about the men?" Kit prompted. "What of them, Ned? Show us."

The boy bared his teeth, clearly as frustrated as the rest of them. Then his frown suddenly cleared, and he grabbed Kit's shirt. Alec stepped forward in alarm, but Kit waved him back as Ned tore at the cotton to expose the sunburst tattoo carved over Kit's heart. He jabbed his finger at the mark, then waved again toward the door.

Alec's stomach did a slow, sickening roll, and Robert swore under his breath. The three of them exchanged horrified looks as Ned continued pounding at Kit's chest.

"Sweet Jesus," Robert breathed. "The Sun League is here."

CHAPTER 2

THEY had very little in the way of possessions, so it was easy enough to collect their few belongings and stuff them into a leather pouch. Ned had slipped quietly back out the door lest Oates realize he was missing and come looking for him. Kit wondered fleetingly how Ned had known he was Sun League, and hoped fervently that the boy's master hadn't figured the same out for himself.

Although they had practically no money, Kit insisted that Alec show their gratitude. Ned's eyes had grown round in wonder as Kit pressed a halfpenny into his dirty palm, likely never having seen that amount of money before. He had clung to Kit like a baby to its mother, making soft, sad noises that needed no wit to interpret, and Kit's heart broke to realize that even the small amount of kindness they had shown the boy was probably more than he'd seen in all his wretched life.

After Kit searched the tiny room to ensure they left nothing behind, Robert eased the door open a crack and looked around; when satisfied, he slipped out, and Kit closed the door behind him. He held his breath, counting slowly in order to give Robert time to gain the stables and prepare their mounts.

When he felt a light tap on his shoulder, he took a deep breath and edged out of the room. Alec followed him, crowding so close that Kit could feel warm breath tickling the back of his neck. They had just reached the edge of the kitchen table when Elijah Oates stepped into the room. Oates had insisted that they pay the reckoning up front, so there was no account to be settled, but Kit knew that sneaking out before first light must look suspicious.

Oates's eyebrows arched in surprise before his customary scowl slid into place. "Leaving so soon?" he asked.

Kit could practically see his mind examining all the possibilities.

"Unfortunately so," Alec said smoothly. He gave Kit a small shove to keep him moving, but Kit's step faltered when a shadow fell across his path, and he looked up to find a tall man blocking the way. Even if he had not recognized the man, he would have known the type; there was something in the arrogant set of his mouth and the assuredness with which he carried himself that bore the hallmarks of the Sun League. As it was, he *had* seen the man once before, when he had accompanied a party of Marcus's men on a scouting mission some ten miles to the west of here. Thomas Bennett had not deigned to notice him then, too intent on catching the ear of Stephen Brody, one of Marcus's closest allies, but others in his small band had been more affable, and Kit feared that one of them would suddenly appear and identify him.

"Excuse me, sir," he said politely.

Bennett didn't move, and Kit felt Alec stiffen behind him.

"Well, my lad. Where are you off to so bright and early?" Bennett asked.

"We have business to attend to," Alec cut in, his voice taking on a steely edge that Kit had never heard before.

Bennett's gaze left Kit's face and flickered upward, and he inclined his head as though weighing up what he saw. Kit's heart hammered against his chest as cold dread flooded him, but a moment later, he felt Alec's hand settle on his shoulder, wordlessly steadying him, and he took comfort in the heat and weight of it.

"What business would that be?" Bennett demanded.

"We are wool merchants, sir," Alec replied easily, ignoring Oates's startled expression. "We are on our way to visit the brothers of Tintern Abbey. If you would step aside?" Though framed as a question, the command in Alec's voice was easy to read. Bennett's brows drew together in a frown, and he looked again at Kit, his eyes narrowing suspiciously.

"And this is your boy?" Bennett asked, giving an odd emphasis to the word.

"My apprentice, aye," Alec said. His fingers tightened in warning, and Kit moved his hand slowly to the small of his back, grasping the handle of a jeweled dagger that was housed in a leather sheath at his waist. He knew instinctively that Alec's other hand was hovering over the hilt of his sword.

As the three of them hung together, tension rising like steam between them, Ned suddenly darted into the room, tripped over his own feet and splashed the contents of the chamber pot he was carrying onto Thomas Bennett's dusty leather boots.

Bennett let out a furious bellow and stepped back, lashing out to land a blow that knocked Ned halfway across the room. Kit started to move toward the fallen boy, but again he felt Alec's fingers dig in deeply, stopping him.

Oates blanched, momentarily stunned, then he began to pour out a string of stammered apologies as he fell to his knees in front of the enraged man and started scrubbing at his soiled boots with a corner of his filthy apron. While Bennett cursed and Oates floundered at his feet, Alec shoved firmly, and this time Kit stumbled forward, casting a final glance at Ned, who was cowering in the corner of the room.

The boy lifted his head, and although a bruise was already starting to color his cheek, a triumphant grin lit up his face. Kit sucked in a sharp breath, realizing that Ned had purposefully diverted attention to himself in order to help Kit and Alec escape. He managed a brief nod that he hoped conveyed his gratitude before Alec forcefully propelled him out of the door.

Once outside, he shook Alec's hands off and ran to the stable. Oates had housed and fed the animals well, even as he'd treated their masters so indifferently, and Robert had hastily saddled them and was holding them at the ready. They walked their horses into the courtyard and out past the wooden fence enclosing the inn, only mounting up when they'd reached the dirt road. With a final tense glance over his shoulder, Kit kicked his horse into a trot, tucking in behind Robert, who was urging his own mount to greater speed while trying to maintain a safe pace in the gloom. Alec brought up the rear, and Kit felt it likely that he was experiencing the same itch between his shoulder blades, as though malevolent eyes were watching.

They rode in silence for several miles, only able to breathe easy when the sun began to crest the low hills to the east and light their way, allowing them to spur their horses to a gallop. When they reached a sizable fork in the road, they veered off onto a narrow track heading southeast. Kit had often traveled this area and knew most of the paths that crossed this part of the shire, but he was keenly aware that the Sun League would know these back roads just as well. He realized that he wouldn't feel safe until they had crossed the border and left Salop far behind them. The League would still be about, but it was unlikely that news of Kit's escape would have spread so quickly outside the shire, and there was less chance of running into people who might recognize him.

By the time they felt secure enough to call a halt, Kit's stomach was beginning to rumble with hunger. After a brief discussion, Robert peeled off, heading in the direction of Bayston Hill to forage for food, and Kit dismounted, stretching out the stiffness in his muscles. Alec climbed down more slowly, and Kit hurried to his side.

"Your shoulder is hurting you," he said. Although Robert had done a good job of cleaning and dressing it, the wound Alec had suffered from de Crecy's arrow was still very tender.

Alec waved him off. "It's fine," he said, although it was clear from the pallor of his skin that he was in some pain.

"At least sit awhile," Kit encouraged. He tugged at Alec's hand and led him to the shade of a tall oak tree. He slipped his cloak off and spread it on the dewy grass, and when he looked up, Alec was trying to hide an amused smile.

"I already have one nursemaid to contend with," he said.

Kit felt a blush warm his cheeks. "It's foolish to risk the wound festering," he said gruffly.

Alec shook his head lightly, but he sat down, patting the cloak beside him.

"Don't you think one of us should keep watch?" Kit asked, casting about nervously. They had walked their horses off the track, but the clearing was easy enough to see from the route.

Alec's smile grew wider. "We'll make a Guardsman of you yet," he teased.

Kit scowled and Alec relented. "We'll hear riders long before we see anything," he said. "Besides, Robert will double back a half mile before he hunts up some food. He won't be so easy to follow." The smile played about his lips again. "We've done this once or twice before, you know."

Kit threw up his hands in defeat and joined Alec on the cloak. The heavy wool soaked up the dew, and it already felt damp to the touch, but Alec either didn't notice or didn't care because he leaned back and stretched out, cupping his head in his clasped hands.

The sun was high in the sky now, and the warm air stirred as a faint breeze drifted through the budding trees, carrying with it the fresh scent of pine. Kit felt himself relax into the soft woolen cloak, his eyes drifting shut as he listened to the gentle birdsong overhead and breathed deeply, pulling in the smell of damp earth.

"Your mother will be happy to see you." Alec's quiet voice briefly startled him.

He opened his eyes and glanced at his friend. "It's been a long time," he said.

"And you're sure she'll still be in Stretton?" Alec asked. Kit felt the weight of Alec's eyes on him and shrugged.

"She has nowhere else to go," he said. Before Marcus de Crecy had swept into their lives and taken Kit away, his family had rarely ventured beyond the village boundaries. His parents had both been born in Stretton; his father had died there, killed by de Crecy's men when he would not bend to the Sun League's will, his body left to burn in the fire that had been deliberately set to destroy his forge. His father's charred remains no doubt lay in the quiet cemetery beside St. Laurence Church, interred alongside generations of his kin.

"Three years is a long time, Kit," Alec said. A note of warning made Kit turn his head and look more closely at his friend. There was something guarded about his usually expressive features, and Kit frowned, wondering at the true meaning behind his words. "A lot can happen in that expanse of time, especially when a woman is left to fend for herself...." Alec trailed off.

Kit waited for Alec to elaborate, but he remained silent. Dappled sunlight played across his handsome face, accentuating deep blue eyes that remained fixed on Kit's face. Kit pondered his words, recoiling when the implication suddenly became clear.

"You think she'll turn me in," he gasped. He turned away sharply, but Alec reached and encircled his wrist, tugging until he turned back.

"I'm only saying we should be cautious," Alec hurried out.

"She's my mother, for God's sake!"

"I'm sorry, Kit. I've seen stranger things happen where the Sun League is involved." Alec's voice was conciliatory but firm.

"You know nothing of my mother," Kit said furiously. He wrenched his arm out of Alec's grip and stood up, blood pounding against his temples. "You should get some rest," he said stiffly, turning his back and stalking off toward the horses. Behind him Alec sighed out loud, but he didn't make any move to follow, and when Kit glanced back moments later, Alec was lying on his side, rolled up in the cloak.

Anger churned Kit's gut, combining with hunger to make him feel nauseous. He had fought hard to reconcile himself to his loss when it had become obvious that Marcus was not going to allow him to see his family. The lesson had been carved into his back with a horse whip when Kit had attempted to escape to rejoin them, and together with the threats Marcus often repeated, Kit had reluctantly come to accept that they were safest without him. The ache of their absence had remained with him, though, and he had never stopped wondering how they fared.

He tried to imagine what it must have been like for his mother, losing both husband and son to the Sun League, her livelihood destroyed by fire, her world gutted overnight. Though it had been the cause of all her troubles, the League would have supported her, its control over the shire made possible through an odd mix of coercion and aid, ensuring that the population was terrified, but also indebted for its assistance in hard times. Kit knew that Marcus had reached out to his family, but it had never occurred to him that they might leave the life they knew and start afresh.

A sound made him turn his head, and he watched as Alec unfurled the cloak and struggled slowly to his feet, pain etched on his face from the wound he had taken on Kit's behalf. A twinge of sympathy swiftly turned to remorse as Kit remembered everything Alec had given up to protect him and bring him justice. Alec's words had stirred something painful, but Kit was honest enough to admit that Alec was probably right. He hadn't been home for years; things were bound to have changed.

"I'm sorry—" Kit started.

"I shouldn't have said that—" Alec said, simultaneously.

They both stopped, and a rueful smile twitched at Kit's lips.

"You're right," he said. "Anything could have happened in three years."

"I just want you to be prepared," Alec said kindly. "Chances are the League took care of your family. It's how they maintain support among the people, after all. But you need to consider all the possibilities. I just don't want to see you hurt."

Kit nodded, grateful that Alec didn't hold his churlishness against him. "I know you think it foolish, but I can't leave without knowing they are safe," Kit said quietly. "And I want to say my farewells. There's no knowing if I'll ever see my family again."

Alec lightly stroked his cheek. "Try not to worry about it," he said. "God willing, we'll be in Stretton by early afternoon tomorrow and all will be revealed."

A rumble of hooves interrupted them, and Kit easily recognized that a single rider was approaching. Moments later Robert came into view, swinging his mount off the path and into the clearing before tossing a bundle wrapped in cheesecloth into Alec's hands.

Alec grinned and unwrapped the package. He handed Kit an apple and a hunk of yellow cheese as Robert broke a round loaf of bread into three equal pieces and shared it out. The sharp cheese crumbled on Kit's tongue, and the warm bread was so fresh that it still tasted faintly of yeast. Kit didn't think he'd ever eaten anything so good. He was still chewing hungrily when Robert spoke up, sounding casual, though his words sent a cold shiver down Kit's spine.

"There's word in the village that the League is on the hunt for a runaway," he said, looking between Alec and Kit.

Alec cursed under his breath.

"A party of three Leaguers came through the village yesterday. They were heading toward Cardeston."

"The men who rode in this morning," Alec said with conviction.

"Most likely," Robert agreed. "The village has been warned to be on the lookout for a young man, probably traveling with two companions." His cocked an eyebrow. "The description of us was pretty good, actually," he added dryly.

"Damnation," Alec said. "I hoped word wouldn't have spread quite so quickly."

"The League has a total stranglehold in this area," Kit said.

"Well, the sooner we move off, the better I'll feel," Robert said briskly.

They hurriedly finished the last of the food and mounted up again, then set a steady pace southward. This was the main route from Shrewsbury to Ludlow, and although not overwhelmed with travelers, they encountered enough people to make the journey uncomfortable in places. Wherever possible, they sought out adjacent tracks, even though they might meander several miles out of the way; still, with the surrounding area heavily wooded and often impenetrable, they found they couldn't completely avoid the road. Fortunately, their fellow travelers seemed as disinclined as they were to engage with strangers, and outside of a cordial nod and a few words of greeting, they passed each other without comment.

As the sky darkened, the pale moonlight could no longer penetrate the thick canopy of trees lining the route, and the path became less safe to navigate. Robert called a halt, turning in his saddle as Alec and Kit pulled up behind him.

"We could probably push on as far as Botvyle," he said. "But I'd prefer to camp here overnight and make an early start. We'll draw too much attention to ourselves if we arrive in the middle of the night."

Alec voiced his agreement, and Kit nodded, even though Robert didn't appear to be asking his opinion. They had avoided most habitation after their flight from Shrewsbury and had spent the first two nights under the stars, shivering in the late spring chill. Kit wasn't as used to the conditions as his friends and couldn't say he relished the idea of sleeping on the hard ground after a cold supper of salted cod, but at least Robert allowed them a small fire, which was as comforting at it was warm.

Huddled close together, hunger abated if not fully satisfied, they sat silently, listening to the fire crackle and spit. Kit snuck occasional glances at Alec and Robert; both seemed absorbed as they stared into the flames, and Kit had a sinking feeling that they were thinking about home and the comforts they had left behind. He only hoped that they were not reconsidering their decision to help him. Dispirited, he pulled his cloak more tightly around himself and lay down, drifting into fitful slumber.

When he awoke sometime later, it was to the soft murmur of voices and the glowing embers of the near-dead fire. Without lifting his head, he listened as Alec and Robert conversed, feeling a little uneasy at eavesdropping but knowing that they were more likely to utter truths if they thought he was safely asleep.

"You know me," Alec was saying. "I have a little something tucked away in my boot heel."

"Aye," Robert replied. "It's as I thought. But we'll have to reconsider our finances soon enough."

"What I have will get us to Ludlow," Alec said.

"I presume you plan to visit Jamie?" Robert said, and Kit's ears pricked up at the unknown name.

"You may presume so," Alec replied shortly.

Kit heard what sounded like a low chuckle from Robert, but if he had planned on pressing for more information, something about Alec's weighty silence dissuaded him.

"And you still intend to indulge the boy with a visit to his mother?" Robert asked. Kit noticed that he seemed less belligerent when he spoke to Alec alone, as though accepting of his captain's quirks.

There was silence for a moment; then Alec fetched up a deep sigh. "I know it doesn't make much sense, Robert," he said quietly. "But he needs to know what happened to his family before he can move on."

"Have you warned him what he might find?" Robert asked.

"God knows I've tried," Alec said, his tone pained. "But I don't think he fully understands."

"He hasn't seen what we have," Robert murmured. "Why don't you let me scout ahead? It might make the way easier."

There was a rustle of cloth, and Kit could only imagine that Alec was shaking his head. "I don't want to put you in harm's way," he said firmly. "Let's stick with our plan."

Robert snorted, but he didn't argue. After a moment he broke the silence again. "It's a lot different being the prey rather than the hunter," he said, and even though the words were whispered, Kit could detect the despondency in his friend's tone.

"I'm sorry I dragged you into this, old friend," Alec said, giving voice to the sentiment that choked Kit's heart. "This isn't how I envisaged ending our days with the City Guard."

Robert dismissed the words with an impatient growl. "Arlen's spent the last two years turning us into a pack of toothless lapdogs," he said bitterly. "I'd sooner live by my wits for the rest of my days than jump through hoops for that bastard."

Kit felt sure that Alec graced his old friend with his warmest smile.

"What about the boy, will he thank us after tomorrow? Will he still think we saved him when the road gets harsher?" Robert asked.

Kit froze, certain that Alec had turned eyes on his supposedly sleeping form. "I hope that whatever lies ahead will be an improvement on the things he leaves behind," Alec said softly. "It's as much as we can hope for."

The ensuing hush stretched so long that Kit was sure Alec and Robert had lain down to sleep. He remained awake for hours, watching the bright moon track across the sky and the cold stars twinkling overhead, pondering Alec's muted warning, melancholy seeping into his bones alongside the damp night air.

CHAPTER 3

THE tiny hamlet of Botvyle lay two miles to the north of Church Stretton, and Alec decided that it was a good place to stow Kit and Robert while he rode ahead to search out Kit's family. The last few miles had taken them through the beautiful uplands of Long Mynd, although their horses hadn't appreciated picking their way through the rock and heather strewn across the windswept trail. Neither Kit nor Robert seemed happy to be left behind, but Alec was able to persuade them that a hot meal in the tavern would set them up for what lay ahead.

Church Stretton appeared to be a prosperous community, Thursday obviously being market day. The narrow streets were thronged with carts laden with produce, all making their way to the large square in the center of the village that was surrounded on three sides by neat, timber-framed houses. The church of St. Laurence dominated the area, its solid Norman architecture echoed in countless buildings throughout the shire, particularly along the western border it shared with Wales. Alec was easily able to mingle with the crowds, and the festive atmosphere loosened tongues and made gathering information relatively simple.

He soon learned that Kit's mother was, indeed, still a resident and that she still lived at the forge that her husband had once owned, which had been swiftly rebuilt after the fire. Alec followed the directions he'd been given, and on the outskirts of the village, he came across the new building and was impressed by its size and layout. Whatever privations Mrs. Porter had suffered as a result of her husband's death, poverty and homelessness were not among them. He remained in the shadows, watching intently for several minutes; but if the Sun League had stationed any of its men here, they were hidden beyond detection.

Feeling a momentary pang of remorse, Alec raised his horse's hoof and worked a small stone underneath its shoe, before walking the hobbled animal into the forge's courtyard and calling out for service. A young boy stuck his head out of one of several bays that lined the yard, then disappeared, and a moment later the farrier appeared, wiping his wet hands down the front of his leather apron.

"How can I help you, sir?" the man asked.

"I'm afraid she's come up lame," Alec said, smoothing a hand down his mare's shiny black coat.

"Let me take a look," the farrier said. He raised the horse's leg and tapped her shoe, a frown furrowing his brow. "There, I see it. Just a small stone lodged under the iron. If you can give me a few minutes?"

"Of course," Alec said.

He looked around with interest as the farrier worked swiftly and surely. "I thought this place had been destroyed some years back," Alec said.

"That's right, sir. A terrible affair," the farrier confirmed. "Burnt right down to the ground and the owner along with it."

"It's a remarkable rebuild," Alec said.

The man raised his head and looked around, pride coloring his voice when he said, "That it is."

"Have you worked here long?" Alec asked.

"A little over two years," the man replied. He raised his head and glanced at Alec curiously. "You're not from these parts I take it?"

Alec shook his head, glad when the back door to the adjacent house opened and a young girl crossed the yard, shifting the farrier's attention away from him. She shared Kit's coloring and something of his beauty, and Alec was certain that she was one of Kit's sisters. She smiled shyly as she approached, her face transformed and lovely, and Alec's suspicions were confirmed.

"Mama says you're to come in for lunch as soon as you finish here," she said to the farrier. She then turned toward Alec and ducked a quick curtsy. "If you please, sir. Mama asks that you come up to the house and slake your thirst while you wait."

From the surprised look on the farrier's face, this was not a common request. Alec smiled at the girl and nodded, and she waved a hand, signaling that he should precede her to the house. She had obviously been well schooled, as she refrained from following him in, although the interest in her eyes was clear.

The wooden door swung open as soon as he approached, and he stepped across the threshold, waiting a moment while his eyes grew accustomed to the dim light. Gradually a woman came into focus, one he'd have recognized anywhere as Kit's mother. She had the same thick chestnut hair and hazel eyes, the same clear skin and full lips, though there the resemblance ended. Instead of open, honest features, hers were pinched and grim, the lines around her mouth and the coldness in her eyes betraying a harshness that was completely lacking in her son.

"I know who you are," she said without preamble. "You bring danger to us all."

Alec felt his eyebrows climb. "If you know who I am, then you also know who is traveling with me," he said softly. "He wants to see you."

Mrs. Porter tensed, and she looked about anxiously. "That's impossible," she breathed.

"We would arrange it safely," Alec urged. "Nobody would know."

She shook her head vehemently. "There are always eyes on us," she said. "I will not allow you to bring this threat into my house."

"They've been here already?" Alec asked, sure she knew to whom he referred.

Mrs. Porter nodded. "More than once, and you can be sure they'll return."

"What did you tell them?" Alec asked.

"What could I?" she snapped. "I knew nothing, thank God." She turned her severe gaze on him, and it was startling to see the cold expression from the mirror of a face that had always looked on him with kindness. "De Crecy came himself," she hissed. "He made it quite clear what would happen if anybody was caught harboring my son."

"You remember, at least, that he's still your son?" Alec retorted. He had imagined this conversation in several ways as he'd ridden into the village, but he'd never considered that it would take this course.

Mrs. Porter's eyes flashed with fury. "Do not presume to judge me, Captain Weston," she said icily.

Alec felt a faint shiver up his spine at the knowledge that de Crecy knew exactly who he was and had named him specifically when issuing his threats. He wondered fleetingly what else the man knew about him.

He sketched a small, apologetic bow. "Your pardon, madam," he said formally. "I am not here to cause you distress, but I beg you to reconsider. Your son has not laid eyes on you these three years. It is his fondest hope to see for himself that you are well."

Mrs. Porter stiffened and again her eyes darted frantically around the room. But as Alec watched, her stern expression unexpectedly melted, her softer appearance making her look so much like Kit that Alec started in surprise. She twisted nervously at a ring on her finger and shrugged helplessly. "I had to weigh the life of my daughters against the loss of my son," she said. "God grant that you are never called upon to make such a choice."

Alec inclined his head, suddenly chastened. Behind her carefully constructed façade was genuine anguish. Though he had given up his livelihood and possessions for Kit, it was little compared to the devastating sacrifice this woman had been forced to make.

"We are leaving Salop, madam," Alec said gently. "Would you not like to see your son one last time before he departs?"

Mrs. Porter wrung her hands, despair warring with pragmatism. "He cannot come here," she whispered, as though afraid they could be overheard. "It's too dangerous. Tell him to meet me in the churchyard of St. Laurence at dusk."

"Thank you," Alec said sincerely, bowing his way out. "It will mean everything to him."

A DAMP fog had settled over the village by the time Kit arrived at the churchyard, his heart beating rapidly in anticipation of seeing his mother after so long. Despite Alec's admonitions, it was hard to contain the swell of eagerness that washed through him. Alec had insisted on accompanying him, and Robert was stationed less than half a mile to the south of Church Stretton, with instructions to ride out at full gallop should the two of them fail to join him at nightfall—instructions Kit felt sure he would ignore if he felt Alec had been compromised.

He and Alec were huddled in the wooden porch, hoods pulled over their faces to avoid recognition, even though there were few people about at this hour.

"You're sure she said St. Laurence?" Kit fretted.

Alec wisely ignored the question.

"And she looked well?" Kit asked, though he'd had the answer at least twice already. Alec grunted a response that Kit decided not to examine too closely. "I wonder if my sisters will come?" he murmured.

"Best not get your hopes too high on that score, Kit," Alec warned. "It will be hard enough for your mother to be abroad this time of night."

"And the forge has been rebuilt? Marcus promised me he had looked after my family, but I was never sure whether to believe him."

"It is as I told you," Alec said mildly. Kit had asked the same questions a dozen different ways since Alec had returned, anxious to hear every detail of his friend's visit. It was a mark of Alec's kindness that he bore the repeated interrogation so patiently.

Kit's heart leapt as a figure detached itself from the shadows beyond the church wall and approached swiftly.

Alec stepped in front of him and looked around quickly as the silhouette resolved itself into Kit's mother. When satisfied, Alec stepped aside, and Kit gazed upon his mother for the first time in three years. The first thing he noticed was that she looked older and more careworn than he'd ever seen her, lines etched deeply around her eyes and mouth; then all thoughts fled as she pulled him into a crushing embrace. Kit was vaguely aware of Alec retreating into the depths of the porch, before he gave himself up to the rising tide of joy.

"I didn't think I'd ever see you again," his mother breathed.

Kit tightened his arms for a moment, then released his hold and took a step backward. "Are you well? How are my sisters?"

"We're all well," his mother said. "You'd not recognize Charlotte and Isabella, they've grown so tall."

"I missed them so much," Kit said. "How have you managed these three years? Alec told me you still work the forge."

His mother glanced quickly in Alec's direction. "The League made sure we were looked after. De Crecy sent his men." She looked away again, biting her lower lip. "He's looking for you, you know?" she whispered. "His spies are everywhere."

Kit heard a rustling and felt Alec's presence at his back. "Did you bring them here?" he demanded.

"Alec!" Kit snapped, jerking his head around, but his anger cooled when his mother failed to respond.

He turned back slowly. "Mother?" he asked. "What's going on?"

His mother's mouth tightened into a thin line. "I had no choice," she said, so quietly that Kit had to lean forward to hear her. "Your father was dead, our livelihood was destroyed, you were... gone." She shrugged. "I still had two children to care for."

"What are you saying?" Alec demanded.

"I remarried," she blurted, her eyes fixed on Kit's face. "He learned the trade and helps me run the forge. He's a good provider for your sisters."

Kit caught his mother's hands in his, their iciness chilling him through. "You did what you thought best," he said. "Nobody would fault you for that, least of all me."

His mother looked into his eyes, and a shadow crossed her features. "What is it?" Kit asked, wondering why she seemed so defensive.

"He's Sun League," his mother said, her voice suddenly devoid of emotion. "One of Marcus de Crecy's men."

Kit felt a cold clutch in the pit of his stomach, vaguely aware of Alec cursing softly beside him. He barely recognized his own strangled voice when he asked, "Who?"

"John Talbot," she replied.

"Talbot," Kit whispered. John Talbot had been there the day Marcus had abducted him, and Kit vaguely remembered the man coming and going over the next few months until he seemed to disappear altogether. He had, at least, always shown a degree of kindness, and Kit had missed him when he'd gone.

"They killed your husband and carried off your son, and you allowed them back into your life?" Alec said incredulously.

Kit's mother snatched her hands back and drew herself up straight. "Who are you to pass judgment on my actions?" she hissed. "I was alone in all the world. I didn't have the luxury of spurning help, not with two mouths to feed. What do you know of such things?"

"Accepting their help is one thing," Alec snarled. "Taking one of them into your bed is something quite different. You must have known what de Crecy wanted with Kit...."

"Alec, don't," Kit warned, but his mother waved her hand as though dismissing his caution.

"All I knew was that he'd be fed and clothed and housed. I knew he'd want for nothing—"

"In return for what?" Alec sputtered. "Surely you knew that too!"

"How dare you presume—"

"Did you ever once think about what he was going through—"

"Enough!" Kit's voice cut through the angry recriminations, silencing them both. He looked between their grim faces, sensing in each what they couldn't see in the other. Alec was almost vibrating with incredulity, but equally stirred by compassion; and his mother's bluster was only pretense, covering a deep, abiding shame.

Kit reached and once more folded his mother's hands in his own. She was trembling with what Kit read as fury. "Does your husband know you are here?" he asked gently, though the word stuck in his throat. She dragged her gaze away from Alec's face and shook her head.

"I told him nothing, but I don't doubt that he suspects something is amiss. Your friend is not as subtle as he thinks," she sneered.

Kit held up a staying hand when Alec surged forward. "Will this cause trouble between you?" he asked.

She shook her head. "John's loyalties are to me now," she said, ignoring Alec's muttered expression of disbelief. "He will not go out of his way to inform on you, though I doubt he will lie if pressed."

Kit pulled in a deep breath. "Will you remember me to my sisters?" he asked, his voice unrecognizably distant.

His mother nodded tersely.

"I doubt I will pass this way again," Kit said, watching as her face crumpled and all the pain she'd pushed down over the years seeped through the cracks in her composure. "It's probably best if I don't tell you where we are going," he added gently.

"And these men you travel with? These City Guards. You trust them?" she asked.

Alec snorted in disgust but mercifully held his tongue.

"With my life," Kit replied fervently. "They have risked everything for me."

"De Crecy hunts them too," his mother said, and for the first time, Kit saw real fear in her eyes.

"Do not trouble yourself on that score," Alec cut in coldly. Kit raised an eyebrow in entreaty, and Alec nodded sharply, stepped off the porch, and walked a short distance until out of earshot.

"You will keep safe?" his mother asked, her voice trembling.

"Aye, you can be sure of it," Kit said, trying to offer a reassuring smile.

"I did all for the best, my son," she said fervently. "John kept an eye on you whenever he could. He told me de Crecy seemed to really care for you." Kit pulled her close, and she eventually relaxed against him, her rapid heartbeat hammering against his ribs. "I swear I didn't know things were so... so difficult for you," she stammered.

Kit allowed the words to wash over him, taking comfort from the intent if not the actual meaning. It seemed improbable that she had been wholly unaware of his suffering, especially when her husband was de Crecy's man and had seen Kit's torments for himself. Still, Kit wasn't about to spoil what might be the last moments he ever spent with his mother. "I presume your husband can protect you now?" he asked.

She nodded against his chest.

"Then I am happy for you," Kit said, meaning it from the bottom of his heart. There was no reason she should continue to flay herself with guilt, especially now that he had escaped Marcus de Crecy's grasp.

A low whistle let Kit know that Alec wanted to be off, so he reluctantly eased his mother upright.

"Will you get word to me when you are safe?" she asked.

"If I can," Kit said. "Try not to fret."

She walked by his side as he crossed the churchyard to find Alec already mounted. Bending his head, he planted a kiss on his mother's cool cheek before boosting up onto his horse.

She clutched his knee and clung tightly. "You will take care of my son, sir," she said stiffly, addressing Alec, though her eyes remained on Kit's face.

"I will, madam," Alec replied.

She attempted a smile but failed miserably, and desperate anguish flooded her face. "God keep you both," she whispered.

Alec saluted and turned his horse's head, and Kit gently removed his mother's rigid fingers from his leg and carefully walked his mount past her. The last he saw of his mother, she was standing as still as a stone statue, her expression emptied of all emotion, save for the tears that ran down her cheeks, glistening under the pale half moon.

HALF a mile outside the village, they caught up with Robert, who was sitting astride his horse beside the Ludlow road. His keen gaze flickered between them and seemed to size up the situation in a glance, reading the tension and sorrow that clung to them. He nodded as they rode alongside him, then wheeled his horse, and wordlessly led them south.

CHAPTER 4

THEY rode for an hour through the starlit night until Alec started to recognize the local landmarks and feel more at ease. He had lived in Ludlow for most of his life and knew the surrounding area well, and when he glanced at his companions and saw that gloom was settling in on them, he decided that a good night's rest and a decent meal were needed to raise their weary spirits. There was little chance of a peaceful night if they stayed on the main road, so instead he led them down a long, winding track and into the courtyard of the Blue Boar Inn, a place he knew would provide good service without asking too many inconvenient questions.

The innkeeper greeted them warmly enough, though he didn't ask them their business or where they had come from. He showed them to a clean, comfortable room, promising to have a pallet sent up to add to the two narrow cots already in place. Alec pressed a coin into his hand, asking that he send up a tub and some hot water. Although seemingly an unnecessary expense when resources were so low, it was impossible for him and Kit to use the pump in the courtyard without revealing the markings on their bodies, the telltale signs that would divulge their identities.

Robert rummaged around in his pack and pulled out three crumpled, mud-splattered shirts. "I'll take these to the kitchen," he declared. "Get the girl to boil them for us."

Alec nodded, happily anticipating the feel of clean cloth against his skin after days of sweat and dirt. As Robert left, the innkeeper returned carrying a tin bath, and behind him two young boys hefted a cauldron of steaming water. They deposited both in the middle of the room and departed without further comment, the innkeeper fishing in his pocket and tossing a bar of coarse soap to Kit before he closed the door behind him.

"You first," Alec said. Kit had not spoken a word since leaving Stretton, dejection settling over him like a shroud. Alec set about pouring the heated water into the tub, standing back when the bath was ready to find Kit already stripped out of his grubby clothes. He gingerly dipped a toe into the water, gasping a little at the temperature, then he stepped into the tub and lowered himself slowly, sighing as steam enveloped him.

"Good?" Alec asked.

Kit managed a smile and a nod. His body was folded into the cramped tub, the water barely coming up to his waist, and he shivered slightly as cool air hit his naked chest. Alec slid to his knees beside the bath, took the soap out of Kit's hand, and quickly rubbed it over the young man's back, taking care to avoid scrubbing too hard at the whip marks grooved deeply into his flesh. He felt a familiar tightening in his groin at the feel of Kit's soft skin and lean muscles under his hand.

He absently traced the crude sunburst tattoo that had been carved over Kit's heart, the identifying mark the Sun League cut into all its men.

"It will never fade." Kit's voice brought his eyes up, and Alec looked into his young friend's troubled face. "It's meant as a permanent reminder. I'll always be theirs," Kit said, his soft tone failing to mask the underlying bitterness.

Alec pressed a little more firmly. "They mark you on the surface because they can't reach inside you," he said. He tapped the center of the tattoo, right over Kit's heart. "They can't control what's there," he said.

Kit smiled sadly. "The Sun League destroys what it can't control," he said. "I don't know how much damage they've already done."

The carnal craving that had stirred Alec's prick suddenly vanished, leaving behind a vague sense of shame. Kit's experience of life so far was of pain and betrayal. It would take time and patience to show him that anything else existed.

"Let's get you finished up," Alec said, hoping to distract Kit from his melancholy. "I want the water while it's still warm."

When Robert returned to the room ten minutes later, carrying a fresh jug of hot water, Kit was redressed and sitting on the edge of the bed, knocking the dust off his boots, and Alec had just wrapped the damp drying sheet around his clean body after climbing out of the tub. He pulled on his clothes while Robert dumped the contents of the jug into the bath, then hurriedly shucked his garments and climbed in. Alec hid a smile as Robert gave himself a quick, efficient wash, seemingly indifferent to the pleasure of warm water, even after days in the saddle.

Feeling refreshed and relaxed, Alec led his companions down the winding staircase and into the brightly lit room that served as a dining hall. Out of habit, he cast around the room, seeing nothing in his fellow travelers that caused concern. Supper was plain but hearty, and it was obvious that Kit and Robert were enjoying it as much as he was, if their silence as they demolished the meal was any indication. Alec made decent inroads into his own heaping plate of spiced eel before slowing down enough to consider conversation.

"Have you thought much about where we'll go when we leave Ludlow?" Robert asked, wiping his greasy lips with the back of his hand. "I presume you'll not want to inconvenience Jamie more than necessary."

"Who's Jamie?" Kit asked. Alec's gaze flickered quickly to Robert's face before landing back on Kit's.

"An old friend," he said, careful not to place too much emphasis on the word. A hint of a smile played about Robert's lips, but Alec didn't elaborate. In truth, James McEwen had once been considerably more than a friend, but Alec didn't want to overburden Kit with information too soon. Kit's eyes were focused on his face, his gaze thoughtful and intent and patently curious.

"I was thinking about London," Alec said brightly, hoping to deflect the young man's attentions.

Robert snorted. "London is not only prime Sun League territory, it's also Anthony Arlen's seat. Isn't that like walking into the lion's den?"

"London is big enough to hide a dozen renegade City Guards and League runaways," Alec responded, smiling slightly. "It's our best hope."

"If you say so," Robert muttered, looking wholly unconvinced. Alec risked another glance at Kit, whose steady gaze was still fixed on him.

"Do you have any thoughts on the subject?" Alec asked. As he suspected, Kit was startled by the question, enough to distract him from pursuing inquiries about Jamie McEwen.

"I've never set foot out of the shire," Kit said.

"Then you have a world of wonder ahead of you," Alec declared, shooting Robert a hard look when the man muttered, "He certainly does," under his breath.

WITHOUT Kit's body rubbing innocently up against his, and secure in the knowledge that the innkeeper would alert him if other travelers wandered in during the night, Alec slept soundly for the first time since lighting out of Shrewsbury. He awoke to find the sun already high in the sky and shooting bright, warm shafts into the room. Kit and Robert were already up and dressed in the shirts that the kitchen maid had scrubbed and boiled the previous day; both looked rested and happier than they'd seemed in days.

Stretching luxuriantly, Alec closed his eyes against the sunshine, enjoying a moment of peace. He heard Robert tell Kit that he was going out, then the door opened and closed softly, and he just about managed to crack an eyelid when the straw-filled mattress dipped and Kit murmured, "Do you intend to sleep the day away?"

A smile twitched his lips. "Maybe just another five minutes," he said hopefully.

Kit laughed, a joyful sound that thrilled Alec's heart. It was good to see that the melancholy shadows that had gathered around Kit were slowly dissipating as the natural buoyancy of youth asserted itself.

"I think you'll like Ludlow," he said. "I spent many a happy year there when I was your age."

"With James McEwen?" Kit asked, his ordinarily open expression carefully neutral.

Alec started slightly, wondering for a moment whether Robert had said more than he should, then instantly dismissing the notion; Robert would never speak out of turn about private matters. It was clear that Kit had picked up on the undercurrents that had flowed between Alec and Robert, and that his natural curiosity wouldn't be satisfied until he'd had the whole story. Fortunately, time was not on their side, so Alec sidestepped the question with nothing more than a brief nod.

"Would you fetch my clean shirt?" he asked. "Robert will have my hide if I'm still abed when he returns." Kit's eyebrows climbed at Alec's obvious equivocation, but he obediently rose and fetched the shirt without further questions.

After they had broken fast with a delicious roast capon, Alec parted with almost half his remaining store of coin, fully aware that the innkeeper's agreeable cooperation came at a price. The money didn't buy his silence, only guaranteed that he would give them a head start before selling their destination to the highest bidder. For that reason, Alec made great show of heading north when they left the Blue Boar, only doubling back to their original route when they were several miles up the road.

He had always loved the gently rolling countryside around Ludlow, and even with two enemies at his back, Alec felt happy anticipation flood him as the warm sun inched over the green hills that stretched westward into Wales. They crossed the fast-flowing River Teme at Bromfield, and less than an hour later they were trotting through the hamlet of Priors Halton and catching their first glimpse of Ludlow through the budding trees.

Raised on a heavily wooded hillock, the town could be clearly seen for miles around. Approaching from the north, Ludlow was framed by the square tower of St. Laurence Church on the left, and the vast limestone castle compound on the right. For more than two centuries, Ludlow Castle had dominated the surrounding countryside, first as a Norman fortress under the command of the de Lacy family, then in recent years greatly expanded by the ambitious Roger Mortimer.

It had been a little over three years since Alec had ridden out of this town, with Robert at his side, and it was with mixed feelings that he rode back in through Linney Gate, the high walls that encircled the town enclosing him like an embrace.

He led them down Broad Street, past fine timber and stone houses that boasted the wealth of their owners, past wool merchants and cloth sellers and the more reputable coaching houses that lined the street. When they turned onto the cobbles of St. John's Road, Alec slowed his mount, then came to a halt across the road from an impressive gray stone house. His eyes remained focused on the large shuttered casements as Robert and Kit drew abreast of him.

"What now?" Robert asked.

Alec glanced sideways and shrugged. "Now, we wait."

AS DARKNESS fell and the last rays of sunshine faded, Kit pulled the hood of his cloak up over his head and rubbed his gloved hands together, trying to encourage some warmth into his cold limbs. They had spent the last two hours in the shadow of a tall building, their eyes glued to a house across the street that clearly held some significance for Alec. Robert had disappeared at one point and returned with a hot meat pasty that had temporarily filled the growling hole in Kit's hungry stomach, but apart from that, they had not moved off this spot. Kit was beginning to sincerely dislike this leg of their journey. It didn't help that nobody would tell him what they were waiting for or what importance the house held.

Alec had stood as though transfixed, his eyes never straying from the cold stone facade. Robert had spoken to him once, close-up against his ear so Kit couldn't hear what had been said. But Alec had simply nodded distractedly and returned to his vigil. Robert had given up with a sigh, and now stood shoulder to shoulder with Alec, eyes turned on the great house, his own gaze fixed and unchanging.

Kit had just about decided to leave the two of them to their sport when Alec suddenly stiffened beside him, sucking in a sharp breath. Kit looked toward the house and saw a carriage pull up and a figure alight and climb the stairs. A moment later, the great front door opened and the figure disappeared inside, and soon the windows were aglow with lamplight, and the house didn't look quite so cold and imposing.

Then it was as if a spell had been broken; Alec finally moved, swiveling his head from left to right as though seeking information in the gathering gloom. Robert took up their horses' reins and tugged the animals after him as he crossed the street, stopping in front of the house to tether the horses to a hitching post. Kit followed Alec as he, too, crossed the street, drawn to the house like a moth to a flame.

They climbed the steep stairs, and Robert lifted the iron lion's head knocker and hammered it against the wooden door until it slowly creaked open and a gray head peeked out. The elderly man's frown was soon replaced by a broad smile as he looked from Robert to Alec.

"By God, Captain Weston!" he declared. "Come in, come in. Welcome home, sir."

Kit felt a jolt of surprise. He followed blindly as Alec disappeared into the house, stopping to shake the old man's hand as he passed. "Francis, you remember Robert Warren?"

"Of course," Francis said. "You are most welcome!"

"And this is Kit Porter," Alec said, waving in his direction. Kit felt a moment of discomfort to hear his name bandied about so easily in front of a stranger, but then, it was becoming increasingly apparent that Francis was no stranger to either Alec or Robert.

"Excellent timing, sirs," Francis said. "The master has just arrived home. He'll be so pleased to see you both. Will you be so good as to follow me?"

He led the way down a long hallway, its walls lined with portraits of what Kit presumed were family members, until he reached a double doorway. Knocking quietly, he pushed open one side of the door and ushered Alec inside. As Kit followed, he was immediately struck by the sumptuousness of the room. A huge stone fireplace took up the whole of the far wall, and everywhere he looked, Kit saw rich furnishings and intricate tapestries; all the surfaces were covered in books and parchment scrolls, and every nook and cranny seemed to overflow with curious objects that Kit knew he'd want to examine more closely if allowed.

He heard a surprised gasp and turned his head to find a man sitting behind an enormous desk, his eyes round with wonder as they swept between Robert and Alec, before settling on Alec's face.

"Look who's here, sir," Francis exclaimed.

"Hello, Jamie," Alec said softly, confirming the identity of the man.

James McEwen stood abruptly, walked around the desk, and vigorously shook Robert's hand before stopping in front of Alec and staring at him as though not quite believing his eyes. Then he suddenly grinned in pure delight and wrapped Alec in an embrace, pulling him so close that Kit wondered how Alec was able to breathe.

As the two men clung together, Kit took a moment to consider James McEwen. He appeared to be of an age with Alec, possibly a year or two younger. He was half a head taller than the captain, though a little leaner through the shoulders; intelligent eyes and a quick smile softened what might otherwise have been a somber face.

He was beautifully dressed in a rich green silk shirt that matched the color of his eyes, and a finely embroidered tunic of soft gray wool. His dark hair hung about his shoulders, curling wildly, and Kit felt a momentary stab of regret that he had chopped his own mane off, especially when Alec ran a thick strand of it through his fingers and pushed it off McEwen's face before brushing a kiss against the man's clean-shaven cheek.

Jamie stepped back a pace and held Alec at arm's length. "It's so good to see you, Alec," he breathed. He looked at Kit expectantly.

"Jamie, this is Kit Porter. He's a friend," Alec said.

Jamie raised an eyebrow, but he simply smiled and held out his hand. Kit shook the hand, surprised by the strong grip, as Jamie said, "I'm pleased to meet any friend of Alec's. May I call you Kit?"

Kit nodded, feeling oddly tongue-tied in front of this handsome man who clearly meant a good deal to Alec and Robert.

"I hope you intend to stay a few days," Jamie said.

"If it wouldn't put you out too much," Alec replied.

"You know you are always welcome, Alec." Jamie smiled, warmth suffusing his face. Kit felt a strange stirring at the affection he read between the two men, and couldn't help but wonder how deep it ran.

Jamie nodded to Francis, who hurried out of the room, then waved the three of them into nearby seats. Kit tried to perch on the edge of a silk-covered sofa, but it was so comfortable that soon he found himself relaxed amongst its deep cushions. Alec didn't fare much better at the other end of the sofa, though Robert remained stiff and alert, seated on a high-backed wooden chair that he pulled away from the warm circle of the glowing fireplace.

"So, what brings you back to Ludlow?" Jamie asked, his eyes fixed on Alec's face.

"I have a little business to attend to. I'm hoping for some guidance," Alec replied.

Jamie nodded. "You know I'll do what I can," he said softly. From the looks that Alec and Jamie exchanged, Kit was certain that

Jamie knew something of their complicated situation. As though reading his mind, Jamie's next words confirmed Kit's suspicions, even as they sent a chill through him.

"I heard your name spoken about town yesterday," he said.

Beside him, Alec stiffened, and Robert leaned forward in his seat. "Anything I should be worried about?" Alec asked. His tone was nonchalant enough, but Kit could hear the undercurrent of anxiety that colored the words.

"Nothing to concern yourself with just yet," Jamie said, waving his hand. "But I'd suggest keeping a low profile while you're here, and I don't think you should plan on too long a stay."

Alec inclined his head. "We'll be on our way as soon as I settle my accounts," he said.

At that moment the door reopened and Francis walked back in, carrying a tray with four steaming glasses balanced on top of it. He quietly circled the room, offering the tray to each of them. Kit took one of the glasses and sipped gingerly at the herb-scented, deep red liquid, sighing in pleasure as a measure of hot, spiced wine slid down his throat. He drank it down eagerly, licking his sticky lips after each hearty gulp, feeling tendrils of heat radiating through him, warming him from the inside out.

The firelight flickered, wooden logs snapping as flames consumed them, and Kit settled deeper into the soft silk cushions. A clock chimed somewhere in the house, and the soft murmur of voices soothed his troubled heart; the coldness and fear that had been his constant companions for the past several days drifted away, and the tension that had stiffened his muscles eased slowly. His eyes drifted shut for a moment, then a moment longer; then blissful peace descended.

Kit wasn't sure how long he'd dozed when he felt a hand shake him gently. He opened his eyes and bolted upright, but the hand eased him back, and over his head he heard a soft chuckle.

"I think your young friend needs his bed."

Kit blinked and looked up to find Jamie McEwen bending over him, concerned green eyes sweeping his face.

"I'm sorry, sir," he stammered, feeling a heated blush spread across his cheeks.

The young man smiled warmly. "It's Jamie," he said. "I'd like to think that any friend of Alec and Robert's is a friend of mine."

Kit nodded, dumbfounded again in the face of Jamie's dazzling appearance and obvious kindness.

"Francis, why don't you see these gentlemen up to their room?" Jamie said. Francis materialized at his side, and Kit struggled to his feet, glancing around to see that Robert and Alec were standing by the door waiting for him, a small smile touching Alec's lips.

"I've given you the blue room at the top of the house," Jamie said. "I presume you want to stay together. But if you'd prefer a different arrangement...." He trailed off, his eyes once more fixed on Alec's face.

"The blue room will be fine," Alec said. "We appreciate your hospitality."

"Come and find me when you've settled in," Jamie said. "We should discuss your business as quickly as possible."

Francis led the way up a flight of stairs, and Kit looked around with interest when they reached the upper floor. The hallway stretched to the left and right, with several closed doorways lining its impressive length. More paintings hung from the papered walls, mostly well-dressed, serious men on horseback, although at the end of the hall was a full-length portrait of a woman, her startling green eyes and great beauty leaving Kit in no doubt that she was related to Jamie McEwen in some way. Unlike Jamie, her green gaze was cool and aloof, and her tight-lipped expression gave the impression of severity.

"Jamie's mother."

Though Alec's voice was no more than a murmur in his ear, Kit thought he detected a coldness that was surprising given how affectionately Alec had greeted Jamie. He looked around in time to see the distaste that briefly flitted across Alec's face before he schooled his expression and turned his head. Kit glanced back at the portrait, struck by how little she looked like her son, despite sharing many of his features.

"Step lively, lad," Robert barked, coming up behind him and giving him a small shove to get him moving. Kit turned and hurried after Francis's retreating back, astonished to see him pull back a heavy tapestry at the far end of the corridor to reveal a small wooden door that opened onto another staircase, this one narrow and dark. He climbed the stairs quickly, Robert hard on his heels, and stumbled across the threshold into a large, surprisingly airy room.

The walls were painted pale blue, clearly giving the room its name. Even though it contained three beds, a desk, several chairs, and a huge wooden chest, the room still seemed spacious, and Kit figured it probably covered at least half the area of the main house. The ceiling consisted of oak beams overlaid with thatch, indicating that the room was tucked up under the eaves. There was only one window, a narrow opening overlooking the alleyway that ran along the eastern side of the house, and Kit judged that from the outside, it would be hard to detect the presence of this room. Given the way it was concealed within the house, he guessed that its hidden nature was its chief recommendation.

The room was aglow in lamplight, and the furnishings were rich and comfortable, yet it was hard to shake the feeling of unease that swept over Kit as Francis left the room and closed the door behind him.

"It's merely a precaution, Kit," Alec said, easily reading his face. "Just until we see the lay of the land."

"Better to be safely out of the way in case of unwanted visitors," Robert chimed in.

Kit swallowed hard but nodded wordlessly; there were certainly worse places to be, as the three of them had already discovered.

Robert pointed to the bed farthest from the door. "You should get some sleep," he said. "Things have a way of looking brighter after a night of rest."

Kit crossed the floor and began to undress. He was disappointed that he wouldn't be sharing a bed with Alec; he'd come to depend on the comfort of Alec's warm body next to his. Still, sliding between the clean, fragrant sheets was a real pleasure, and he'd just snuggled under the soft woolen blankets when the mattress dipped, and he looked up to find Alec perched on the edge of the bed.

"It will only be for a few days while I sort out my affairs," Alec said.

"It's fine," Kit said quickly. He couldn't explain the apprehension that this place elicited in him and just hoped that his friends didn't think he was being ungrateful. "What do you need to sort out?" he asked.

Alec glanced away, his shoulders stiffening. "It's nothing for you to worry about." He reached out and patted Kit's hand. "Get some rest," he murmured. "Tomorrow will likely be a busy day." He rose and walked toward the door, stopping briefly to exchange a word with Robert before he left. Kit's eyes remained fixed on the wooden door long after Alec had closed it behind him.

"You can trust Jamie McEwen, you know." Robert was sitting on the bed closest to the door, pulling off his boots. "They go back a very long way," he added.

"I do trust him," Kit said, fairly certain that the words he'd spoken were true.

"Alec knows Ludlow like the back of his hand," Robert continued. "And he has a lot of friends here. He'll be safe."

Kit was grateful for the reassurance, and after saying good night to Robert, he settled back under the covers, resolutely ignoring the apprehension that still niggled at him.

THE house was just as Alec remembered it, right down to the fragrance of orange rind and rose petals that sweetened the air. Memories crowded in, bringing a fond smile to Alec's face, a smile that faded as the portrait of Mrs. Alexander James McEwen rose into view. She was a handsome woman—Jamie owed his fine features to her—but the resemblance between them was only perfunctory. There was a warmth to Jamie that was wholly lacking in his mother, a vibrancy that transcended the air of distracted melancholy that sometimes clung to him and gave him a liveliness that she would never possess. Her icy eyes seemed to follow Alec as he crossed the hallway to the staircase, and he felt her painted gaze on him, like a chill, long after he had turned his back on her portrait and bounded down the stairs.

Jamie was still in the study, standing in front of the great fireplace, gazing distractedly into its dancing flames. He turned when Alec entered the room, a smile on his lips that warmed his cool green eyes.

"It's so good to see you, Alec," he said. "It's been too long."

Alec crossed the floor and briefly cupped a hand to Jamie's flushed cheek. "Aye, it has," he murmured. "You look well."

Jamie waved him into a seat, pulled up a chair opposite, and sat so close that their knees touched. He leaned in, looking unusually grave. "You don't have much time," he said softly. "Your name is on the wrong lips. It's too dangerous for you in Ludlow."

"Who's talking, and what are they saying?" Alec asked.

Jamie shrugged. "Within the city walls, it's the Guard, outside it's the League. Whatever you've done seems to have offended both parties."

"And what do they say I've done?" Alec pressed.

Jamie arched an eloquent eyebrow. "Some of the Guardsmen speak of betrayal," he said. "The League speaks of retribution. What are you mixed up in, Alec? I presume it has something to do with your young friend?"

Alec glanced away. "I need your help, Jamie," he said softly, avoiding the question. "I need to realize some funds very quickly. We have to escape the shire as soon as possible."

Jamie inclined his head, considering Alec closely. "Are you sure you need to take such drastic action? Perhaps this will all blow over in a week, a month...?" he trailed off hopefully.

Alec shook his head. "As you say, I've provoked two very powerful camps. There's no going back."

Jamie sighed heavily. "I have some contacts. It will take a few days to put things into place, but I should be able to sort something out for you."

Alec smiled, relief momentarily edging out the anxiety that had dogged him for days. "Thank you," he said sincerely.

Jamie just waved him off. "Are you going to tell me what trouble you've found for yourself?" he asked.

Alec smiled tiredly. "Can we leave that for another day?" he asked.

Jamie reached over and patted his leg. "Tomorrow will be time enough," he agreed. He rose and crossed the room, then stopped beside a table and poured wine from a decanter into two crystal glasses. He returned to the fire and handed one of the glasses to Alec before lifting his own in salute. "To old friends," he said, a smile once more touching his lips.

The wine was rich and mellow, its full-bodied flavor rolling pleasantly over Alec's tongue. He drank deeply, savoring the taste of sunshine, enjoying the warm flicker of the fireplace and Jamie's quiet, supportive presence. Standing, he carried his glass with him as he toured the familiar room. Jamie's family had been merchant traders for many generations, and through the years they had amassed an eclectic collection of curios and oddities, most of which had ended up in this study.

Alec wandered over to the carved mahogany desk that dominated the north end of the room. A huge ledger was spread open, its pages ruled and filled with cramped but neat script. He had a sudden, sharp recollection of standing beside the desk as a youngster, Jamie's sticky fingers laced in his, silently watching Jamie's father make careful entries into the ledger, keeping a record of the comings and goings of his small fleet of trading vessels and the increasingly complex roster of goods they carried. He raised his head and caught Jamie watching him, a wistful smile on his face as though he, too, conjured the scene. The memory, though sweet, was accompanied by a sharp stab of regret, still bitter, despite being tempered by the passage of time.

His fingers drifted across the desk to stroke the spine of a sumptuously bound book.

"This is new," he said.

Jamie's smile broadened. "You have a good eye," he said, crossing the room. He carefully opened the volume to reveal a beautifully illustrated psalter, brilliant hues of red and blue and delicate gold leaf all but leaping off the pages. "I picked it up on my last trip to London," he said, adding quietly, "It's a gift for my mother."

Alec felt his gut tighten. "How is she?" he asked politely, his eyes drawn to his friend's handsome profile.

Jamie snorted. "As always," he replied. "She's visiting her sister in Hereford. I expect her back within a few days."

Alec nodded briskly. There was precious little love lost between himself and Mrs. McEwen, and he silently resolved to conclude his business here as quickly as possible and save them both from what was sure to be an unpleasant encounter.

"She no longer blames you, Alec," Jamie said softly.

"Am I supposed to feel grateful for that?" Alec said, more sharply than he had intended. He was immediately sorry for his flash of temper when he saw Jamie wince. "It's in the past," he said quickly. "I no longer think on it." It was a lie, but one that seemed to bring some peace to his friend.

"We'll speak no more of it," Jamie said, obviously grateful for the reprieve. "Robert is still with you, then?" he continued, deftly steering the conversation to surer ground.

Alec chuckled. "I'd be lost without him," he said warmly. "Though God knows, he'd be better off going his own way."

"He's steadfast," Jamie said. "You always inspired loyalty in your men. It's why you still have many friends in the Guard. They haven't all turned against you."

"That's a relief," Alec said. "I might need their help before my visit here is over."

Jamie shook his head. "Just be careful," he counseled. "There's speculation that a bounty is about to be posted on your head. Friendship is all too easily set aside for the right price."

Alec clapped a hand on Jamie's shoulder. "Not all friendship," he said.

"You're just lucky I don't need the money," Jamie countered, his eyes twinkling with mirth.

Alec laughed out loud and leaned toward his friend, placing a chaste kiss on his flushed cheek. "I'm very grateful, Jamie," he said. "Whatever your motivations." He tossed the remaining wine down his throat, enjoying the last of the rich flavor and the accompanying lightness in his head. "If you don't mind, I think I'll turn in for the night. It's been an eventful few days."

"Of course," Jamie said. "Why don't you join me for breakfast? You can fill me in on your adventures."

"I'll see you bright and early," Alec agreed. "Good night, my friend."

He turned and left the room, and when he gained the hallway, he purposefully averted his eyes from the portrait of the woman who had hounded him from Ludlow and poisoned the purest love he had ever known.

CHAPTER 5

ROBERT had been right; things did look a whole lot brighter to Kit the next morning.

He hadn't heard Alec coming to bed the night before, and both his friends were already up and out of the room when he woke after a deeply satisfying sleep. Kit stretched lazily, watching long tendrils of sunlight slant across the room through the narrow window, illuminating the motes of dust that floated in the air.

At first he couldn't pinpoint the cause of the unsettled feeling that suffused him, until it dawned on him in a sudden, brilliant flash of clarity that made him bolt upright.

He was alone.

Marcus wasn't beside him demanding attention, the room wasn't swarming with rowdy men loudly pursuing their own aims, he wasn't ensnared by the countless sharp eyes that had followed his every move for the past three years. Although the initial rush of exhilaration at his newfound freedom was heady, Kit found it strangely disconcerting to have nobody to tell him what was expected of him.

He rolled out of bed and pulled on his clothes, then hurried down the staircase to find the door at the bottom open and the heavy tapestry pulled back to allow him through. Walking quietly down the long hallway, Kit cocked his head, listening intently for any sign of life. The house was eerily silent, until he heard the sound of somebody moving about downstairs. Unsure of what to do or where to go, Kit crept down the staircase to the ground floor and poked his head around the study door, smiling shyly when Jamie McEwen caught sight of him and called out a greeting.

"Come in, lad," Jamie said. "I'm afraid you missed breakfast, but I'm sure my steward can find you something to eat."

Francis appeared behind Kit as though out of nowhere, nodding briefly toward his master before disappearing again. Kit edged his way into the room, grimacing when he brushed up against a heavily laden table, loudly jostling its contents. He felt an embarrassed flush warm his cheeks as Jamie turned a sweet, sympathetic smile on him, pretending not to notice his clumsiness.

"My father found that in Spain," he said, pointing toward the table Kit had disturbed.

Kit turned his head, his mouth gaping open at the sight of a small, jeweled cage containing what looked like a golden bird, complete with delicate filigree feathers. Jamie crossed the room and picked up the cage, turning it upside down for a moment, then righting it before setting it back on the table. Kit was startled to see the bird's head move from side to side, then watched in awe as its beak opened and a trilling song filled the room.

"Is it alive?" he breathed, his eyes round with wonder.

Jamie's smile grew wider. "No. See here, it was crafted in Toledo by a master goldsmith."

"How does it work?" Kit asked, gingerly fingering the bars of the gilded cage.

Jamie shrugged. "It's an ancient technique, passed down from the Muladi. My father said this particular specimen was unique in design. He parted with a small fortune for it."

"It's beautiful," Kit said. His hand drifted to the hilt of a dagger lying on the table beside the cage.

"Also from Toledo," Jamie said. He picked up the stiletto and held it out to Kit. The handle was smooth and warm, with a tiny star carved into the dark ebony wood; the steel blade glinted, its edge carefully honed and finely serrated to inflict maximum damage. "This knife is said to have belonged to one of the ancient kings of Castile," Jamie said.

"You have so many wonderful things," Kit said, his gaze flickering around the room and lighting on one amazing object after another.

"My family has a long history of trading," Jamie said. "And none of us can resist the unusual or exotic. You're very welcome to look around."

Kit murmured his thanks, then stepped back as Francis returned to the room bearing a tray loaded with steaming food. He placed the tray on a low table beside the sofa, careful to shift several scrolls out of the way first, then beckoned Kit over. At first Kit felt awkward, picking over the dishes by himself while Jamie looked on, but, as if aware of his discomfort, Jamie pulled up a chair and began to help himself, encouraging Kit to tuck in more heartily. The food was delicious, fish and fowl he'd eaten many times, but with flavors he had never tasted before. A dish of carp produced a burst of unexpected heat that had Kit reaching hurriedly for his tankard of small ale.

"We use spices from the Orient," Jamie said. "We import them through Venice."

Kit swallowed a great gulp of the cool ale and wiped his mouth with the back of his hand. His lips and tongue tingled, but the feeling was not unpleasant.

"You must travel a lot," he said.

"Not nearly as much as I'd like to," Jamie laughed. "But I've seen most of the great trading cities, Venice, Genoa, Alexandria. Does travel hold any interest for you, Kit?"

"I've never really considered it," Kit replied, his hand unconsciously rising to cover the tattoo that was carved into his chest. He had long ago given up making any plans for himself. Being under the control of Marcus de Crecy and the Sun League meant that his life was not his own; it had been both pointless and painful to hope that anything could exist for him outside of doing Marcus's bidding.

"Alec told me a little about your... circumstances," Jamie said gently.

Kit tightened his fingers reflexively. He glanced up at Jamie's face, reading compassion in the deep green eyes. He was surprised at the sense of shame that flooded him; after three years of base servitude under the twisted tutelage of Marcus de Crecy, he hadn't been aware that he had any pride left to wound.

"He didn't betray your confidence," Jamie hurried to add. "I needed to know what you were up against so that I could provide the best help."

Kit swallowed hard, fighting down the sting of humiliation. He nodded wordlessly, afraid that if he opened his mouth, he would say something that he might later regret.

"Alec is a man of principle," Jamie continued. "I can think of no better person to entrust your future to."

There was something in the despondent undercurrent of Jamie's words that pulled Kit out of his introspection. It had become apparent that Alec meant a great deal to Jamie, though Kit still wasn't exactly sure where they stood in each other's lives. He pulled in a calming breath, feeling some of his discomfort ease. Jamie had offered them shelter without question, unwittingly putting himself in danger; it was only right that he know something of the situation that had brought them to his door.

"I've not had much occasion to consider the future," Kit said carefully, glad that his voice held steady. "But I imagine seeing the world would be a fine life."

"There are hardships in all the choices we make," Jamie replied, the melancholy in his voice hinting at the personal truth behind the words. "But I think in this case, the good outweighs the bad." He rose suddenly. "I have to meet Alec to sort through some business, and Robert is out on his own errands. You are most welcome to explore the house and grounds while we are away."

Kit felt disappointment rise. "Can I not venture abroad?" he asked. He'd spent so many years either shackled to Marcus's side or constantly watched over by de Crecy's men, and he yearned to taste the freedom of being alone in a new and exciting place.

But Jamie frowned and shook his head. "Alec asked that you remain here until he returns," he said apologetically. "Ludlow teems with people from all parts; he worries for your safety."

Kit bit his lip but nodded his acceptance.

"I'm sure you'll find something to interest you here," Jamie said, waving his hand around the study. "And Francis will see that all your needs are met. We'll return as soon as possible."

"Thank you, sir," Kit said. "Jamie," he amended quickly at the young man's raised eyebrow. "I would like to take a closer look." In truth, the room was so filled with intriguing objects that Kit didn't mind passing a few hours here, and he'd be alone, something he was eager to test.

"I'll tell Francis not to disturb you, then," Jamie said, once again seeming to read his thoughts. "Just ring the bell if you need anything." He turned and left the room, closing the door firmly behind him.

Kit listened to his footfalls until they disappeared, leaving behind a keen hush such as Kit had rarely experienced before. He glanced around the study, scarcely knowing where to begin, then shrugged and unrolled the scroll closest to hand.

He didn't know how much time passed before the door opened again, so enthralled by the jumble of papers and the sheer volume of items that filled the room that he was unaware of the hours ticking away. He was poring over a particularly vivid map when he became aware that he was being watched. He turned his head, expecting to see

Francis, his heart leaping when he saw Alec standing in the doorway, smiling to see him so engrossed.

"It's an amazing collection, isn't it?" Alec said. "I've lost many a happy hour here myself."

"I've never seen anything like it," Kit breathed, overawed by all he'd seen. There were leather-bound volumes in languages Kit had never read; finely illustrated maps that showed parts of the world he had never heard named; stuffed animals under glass that he recognized as distant kin to the woodland creatures he'd grown up with, although different in size and coloring. There were long inventories listing unfamiliar words and handsome boxes filled with all manner of strange and beautiful objects whose use he could only guess at. There were jeweled daggers and glinting swords and even a crossbow, though Kit had never seen the unusual construction before, nor could he identify the wood it was made from.

"I used to think that one day I'd get to add to the collection myself, maybe find something that the family had never seen before," Alec said wistfully. "Jamie and I had such plans...." He trailed off, shaking his head as though to dislodge the train of thought.

"You planned on taking to the seas?" Kit asked, intrigued by this insight into Alec's carefully guarded past.

"We were just boys," Alec said quickly, dismissing the subject. He turned as the door reopened, looking relieved when Robert walked in. "How did you fare?" he asked.

Robert glanced at Kit. "Some of de Crecy's men are in Ludlow," he said. Kit couldn't quite suppress the shudder that ran though him, and he was inordinately glad when he felt Alec's steadying hand grip his shoulder.

"It was to be expected," Alec said. "I'm sure they are to be found in most of the villages between here and Shrewsbury. What of the Guard?"

Robert frowned. "Not much better news there, I'm afraid," he said. "Arlen has put a price on our heads."

Kit gasped, and Alec squeezed his shoulder more tightly.

"It's enough to make most men stop and consider," Robert said dryly. "But not quite enough to make them stir to find us. Arlen always was a cheap bastard!"

"We may count our blessings for that," Alec said. "I'll need a day or two to conclude my business here, then we'll move on as planned."

Alec turned Kit to face him. "Robert and I will be out and about over the next days. You need to stay out of sight."

Kit opened his mouth to protest, but Alec laid a finger on his lips. "I know it's difficult, but we can work more quickly if we're not worried about your safety. Will you stay in the house? I'm sure you'll find enough here to entertain you."

Kit felt unexpected frustration well up. "I don't need entertaining," he retorted. "I'm not a child to be coddled. I could help, if only you'd allow it."

Alec dropped his hand and stepped away, his jaw tightening as surprise registered on his face.

"Your pardon, I meant no insult," he said. "We're likely to draw attention to ourselves if we walk abroad together, and I fear for you, out by yourself in an unknown place." He stopped suddenly, then nodded. "But you are right—you are not a child," he continued softly. "I can't compel you to stay inside, I can only suggest what I think is the wisest course. For all of us."

His tone was friendly enough, but Kit sensed an underlying uneasiness that made him regret his ill-humored outburst. He opened his mouth to apologize, but Alec turned abruptly and left the room, almost bowling Robert over in his haste.

Robert watched Alec charge blindly out, then turned, a fierce frown darkening his expression. "I'm going to take you at your word and presume that you are not a child," he said coldly. "So I'm going to tell you something that the captain wanted to keep from you. He's selling his house in Shrewsbury in order to finance our escape. Lock, stock, and barrel. Only the merchants here are a canny lot; they can smell desperation on him like a hound scents a partridge. They're only offering him a fraction of what the property is worth. But he's intent on selling anyway, despite my pleas, despite Jamie's advice to the contrary. He's bankrupting himself for you." He stopped abruptly, possibly sensing the shock that Kit felt sure was easy to read on his face.

"I... I had no idea," Kit stammered, shame flooding him.

"His only wish is to keep you safe," Robert said, his tone softening. "Don't make that harder than it should be."

IT HAD rained a little in the afternoon, but the air was surprisingly warm when Kit stepped through a set of doors and into the walled garden at the back of Jamie's house. The aroma of honeysuckle vied with the smell of wet earth as Kit walked along a muddy path that wound its way through formal gardens before ending at a small, grassy hillock sheltered by overhanging trees. Alec was standing in the shadow of one of the trees, dressed in breeches, long leather boots, and a white linen shirt that hung from his frame like a sheet. In his right hand, he balanced a sword, and he was running through a series of movements, looking as lithe as a dancer.

Kit hung back for a moment, noting the concentration that drew Alec's brows together, the clean, graceful lines his body made as it flowed through each set of motions, and the sheen of sweat that darkened Alec's hair and glistened on the exposed skin at his neck. Kit was loath to speak or draw closer, unwilling to disturb the spectacle, but without turning his head or slowing his movements, Alec said, "I'm out of practice." He grunted in exertion as he parried and thrust, all the time moving as though avoiding the attack of an opponent.

Kit wasn't sure he'd ever seen anything so poetic.

"You don't look out of practice," he said, smiling as Alec spun around, the sword slicing downward in one long sweep.

Alec laughed breathlessly. "Ask Robert," he panted. "He's sure to provide a contrary opinion."

Kit continued to watch in fascination, until Alec made one final flurry of moves, then sheathed his sword and bowed with a flourish. "It will do," he said.

Stepping forward, Kit picked up the doublet that Alec had flung over a branch, and held it out. Alec smiled his thanks and slipped his arms into the garment, turning slowly as he laced up the front.

"I'm sorry...."

"I want to apologize...." Kit stopped, realizing that he'd spoken over Alec. He frowned when the meaning of the words sunk in. "What are you sorry for?" he asked. "I'm the one who was rude and ill-tempered."

"I have no right to tell you what to do—"

"You have every right to safeguard Robert and yourself," Kit interrupted. "And you have more experience with these things. Robert is right, I should keep my mouth shut."

"Robert didn't say that," Alec chided.

Kit grinned. "No. But it was clear from his expression that he thought it."

A smile twitched at the corner of Alec's mouth. "I won't gainsay that," he agreed. Then he sobered, looking uncharacteristically grave. He reached out and gripped Kit's shoulders. "I never want you to think you have no say in your future," he said. "You spent too long living the life somebody else forced on you."

Kit shrugged, feeling a jumble of emotions. "I'm not used to thinking about the future," he said softly. "Marcus made it clear that my life was in his gift and that if I stopped pleasing him, he'd have no further use for me. I gave up all my hopes and dreams a long time ago." He winced slightly as Alec tightened his fingers.

"This is your time now," Alec said firmly. "If you disagree with anything I decide, you must say so." A sudden lopsided grin eased the tension out of his face. "As you can see, Robert has no trouble telling me when he thinks I'm wrong. It is a skill you'd be wise to learn from him."

"I'll do my best," Kit said. "And if I were to start by telling you I agree with Robert and Jamie, that you are foolish to sell your property...."

"I'd tell you what I told them," Alec said mildly. "That it is none of your business." He smiled at the crestfallen look on Kit's face. "I didn't promise I'd agree, just that I'd listen," he said. "Look, I appreciate your concern, but I know what I am about. I'll never return to Shrewsbury, I've made my peace with that."

The sudden spasm in Kit's gut told him that despite his best efforts, he'd never really appreciated all the implications of this situation. Alec and Robert were giving up their livelihoods, compromising their safety, and confronting a whole new future for him. He couldn't help wondering if the price they were prepared to pay was worth the pitiful gratitude that was all he had to offer in return.

"GOOD God, man, you have more clothes than any half dozen other men put together!"

Jamie smiled as Alec pulled numerous shirts out of the clothespress in his bedchamber, holding each up while he considered their color and cut. The few articles of clothing that Alec and his companions had in their packs were sorely in need of washing and mending, and Jamie had offered to loan them a few items.

Jamie was sitting in a very comfortable armchair, watching in amusement as Alec picked through a vast selection. "You should be thankful that I do," he said. "It will stand you all in good stead." He nodded to a pale blue silk shirt. "That would do very well for Kit," he said. "It would suit his coloring."

Alec inclined his head, considering the shirt, then signaled his agreement.

"He's a very beautiful young man," Jamie said. "Are you two—"

"I don't know what we are," Alec cut in quickly. "We haven't had much of a chance to find out."

Jamie nodded his understanding. "I suppose it's difficult for him," he said softly. "Given all he's been through."

"Aye," Alec replied. "It will doubtless take some time. What about this one?" He held up a dark green shirt, and Jamie was perceptive enough to follow his lead and change the subject.

"I think it will look very well on you. Try it on."

Without thinking, Alec slipped off the soiled linen shirt he was wearing.

"God's wounds," Jamie hissed.

Alec looked up, startled, then remembered the markings on his body—deep grooves that had been cut into him by a whip some years back, marring his front and back, coupled with the recent livid arrow wound through his shoulder that was still red and raw.

"It's a dangerous business, this City Guard," Jamie murmured. He stood up and reached for the shirt Alec was discarding, helping him out of the tangle of its sleeves. He brushed his fingers lightly over the worst of the raised scars. "We heard you'd been taken by the League," he said.

"I'd barely ridden five miles out of Ludlow," Alec replied, still disgusted at the ease with which he'd been captured. It was true he had been grieving at the time; Jamie's father had recently died, and his passing was as painful a blow to Alec as to his friend, but that was no excuse for the complete lack of caution he'd exercised on the dangerous route to Shrewsbury. "They were waiting in ambush," he continued, ruefully. "Luckily I was rescued in good time."

"But not before they did this," Jamie said, his gaze traveling over Alec's torso. "I remember hearing you'd been picked up. The Guard was forming up rescue parties. I wanted to ride along with them."

Alec smiled wryly. "I can imagine how that sat with your mother."

Jamie winced. "I would have gone anyway, but then we heard that you'd been freed."

"Thanks to Robert," Alec said. "He risked all to save me."

Jamie traced a gentle path down Alec's back, making him shiver slightly. "I didn't know you'd been so ill used," he said, his tone conveying both concern and anger. "You should have come home to recover—"

"Your mother made it plain that this was no longer my home," Alec interrupted. "It's the reason I left in the first place."

Jamie waved a hand. "She would have seen reason," he said. "Her temper cooled as soon as you left. I'm sure she regretted the words you'd exchanged."

Alec patted his friend's arm, hoping to placate him. This was a subject upon which they would never see eye to eye. "It was all for the best," he said, not really meaning it but risking the falsehood in order to spare Jamie's feelings.

Jamie grabbed at his hand, his eyes sparking with emotion. "I'm glad you came back home for help now," he said fervently. "I've missed you."

"I missed you too," Alec said. He knew the deep love he'd felt for Jamie would always be there, no matter how tainted it had become before they last parted. He felt it stir and swell inside him now, looking into the sea-green eyes that so transparently reflected Jamie's feelings. But the love was now tinged with melancholy and loss, and it was impossible to recover the sweetness that had once existed between them. Alec hadn't been sure he would ever find that purity of feeling again, until he'd met Kit Porter.

Jamie squeezed his hand. "I hate to think that you're going to disappear again so soon," he said. "I hope you know that as long as I draw breath, you will always be welcome here."

The grateful smile that tugged at Alec's lips was genuine enough, even though in his heart he knew that he would never again call Ludlow home.

He pulled Jamie's green shirt over his head, once again hiding the ugly markings. The abrasions no longer caused actual pain, but they would always scar him, cut so deeply that they would never completely fade. He had often wondered at the viciousness of the attack on him; the days of torture had seemed so pointless. He had no money and no family connections, there had been little to be gained by kidnapping him, and yet his captors had held onto him for days.

"I'll take these up to Robert and Kit," he said, scooping up a handful of assorted clothing. "We'll see you downstairs."

"It will be just like old times," Jamie said happily.

"Indeed it will," Alec laughed, allowing himself to be seduced by Jamie's infectious enthusiasm and glad that, for one night at least, they would be able to forget their troubles and give themselves up to pleasure without reservation.

"I SCARCELY knew which way to look, and Alec's face was as red as a radish."

The room erupted with mirth, and Alec winked at Robert, acknowledging the laughter at his expense. His friend was in rare form, relaxed and talkative and happy to share stories about past escapades. It was a side he showed very few people, and then only when he felt secure in his surroundings and assured of the company. Robert grinned back at him and lifted his glass in silent salute, before tossing back the contents in one great gulp.

The dining room had grown increasingly warm as the pleasant hours passed, even though Francis had allowed the fire to burn itself out so it was now little more than glowing ash. They had all started the night dressed sumptuously in Jamie's silk shirts and fine woolen breeches, with satin doublets laced up to their necks, but as the evening progressed and the good red wine flowed, they had one by one begun to shed their layers.

Kit had been first, tossing his dark blue doublet onto one of the empty dining room chairs and tugging at the laces on his shirt to expose his throat to the air. Jamie had quickly followed suit, and even Robert had loosened the ties on his doublet and opened the top button on his clean white shirt. Alec had rolled up his shirtsleeves and eventually abandoned his doublet altogether, and now they looked more like a party of farm hands after a long day of toiling the fields and less like the well-dressed gentlemen who had begun the evening.

Alec had eaten at this table for many years, so was used to the vast variety and selection, but he had taken great pleasure in watching Kit and Robert as they sampled each new course, their eyes round with undisguised awe at everything that was placed before them. There were fruits and vegetables such as were rarely seen in England, carried from warm climes on Jamie's fleet of merchant ships; fish and meat prepared with spices that had arrived at these shores after months of tortuous travel from every far-flung corner of the earth; and rich wines from southern Europe, each selected to complement the exotic flavors of the food.

As they finished up a course of stewed rabbit swimming in a thick wine sauce, Alec took the opportunity to fondly contemplate each of the men sitting around the table: Robert, his closest friend, loyal to a fault, with a sly wit and a gruff exterior that masked a deeply caring heart. The candlelight revealed the gray at his temples and flecking his neatly trimmed beard, but the tiny wrinkles that had furrowed his brow had relaxed and years seemed to have melted off his face and vigorous form. Jamie, his first love, who would always have a place in his heart, despite the passing of time and the vagaries of fortune. His lovely face was flushed with wine and animated with enthusiasm, his affectionate nature stirred by his companions, new and old. And Kit, who held the key to Alec's future, serenely beautiful in the flickering firelight and as happy as Alec had ever seen him.

Kit and Jamie had their heads bent closely together as Jamie regaled Kit with stories about the great trading cities. Alec knew instinctively that under other circumstances these two would be the greatest friends: Kit, with his bright, quick wit; Jamie, genuinely compassionate and eager to share his vast knowledge and encourage Kit's endless questions.

An intense light was shining in Kit's eyes as he devoured Jamie's colorful tales of foreign lands. Alec looked at Robert, who raised an eyebrow and glanced toward the two younger men. Earlier, they had briefly discussed a plan Jamie had started to formulate, and Alec knew Robert's mind on the subject and knew he could rely on his friend's counsel if needed.

He waited until Francis had replaced the empty plates with bowls of dried figs and nuts, dishes of green olives, and a wheel of soft French cheese, then withdrawn from the room, closing the great wooden doors quietly behind him. Clearing his throat, he turned toward Kit, acknowledging Jamie's almost imperceptible nod. "You seem intrigued by tales of travel," he said softly.

"It sounds like such an exciting life," Kit said, his face aglow with wonder. "Jamie says there are things out there I've never even dreamed of!"

"Would you like to see for yourself?" Robert asked.

Kit frowned, clearly not comprehending.

"Jamie has a ship bound for Bruges," Alec said. "It leaves next month from the port of Boston in Lincolnshire. He's offered us a berth."

Kit's head swiveled between them, his eyes growing impossibly large. "I've never sailed before," he breathed. "I wouldn't know what to do."

Jamie laughed. "You'd soon pick it up. The basics are pretty easy if you've a mind to learn."

Kit turned to face Alec. "And you'd accompany me?" He gestured toward Robert. "You would both leave these lands?"

Robert shrugged. "What is there to hold either of us here?" he asked. "I've never visited the Low Countries. I can't think of a better time."

"It won't be forever," Alec continued. "Just long enough for things to cool down here and for all of us to earn a little coin. In a few months, we'll return with a new trade under our belts. If we want, we'll be able to start over."

"Or you could continue with your travels," Jamie put in. "My ships sail several times a year to different ports. If you take to the sea, I could always find a berth for you."

Kit looked wholly overwhelmed as a life he'd scarcely dared dream about was suddenly laid out in front of him, beckoning him forward. "You should think on it," Alec said. "It's a big decision."

Kit flashed him a grateful smile. "To see the world," he whispered. "It's beyond imagination."

Jamie leaned in and slipped an arm around Kit's hunched shoulders. "I promise you would not regret it, should you decide to go," he said warmly.

As though on cue, Francis slipped into the room and placed a tray on the table containing four beautiful goblets, each a masterpiece of cut and design. "Murano glass," Jamie said. "There are no better craftsmen in all of Venice. You can watch them at work in the alleyways behind the canals. These were made especially for my family."

Alec picked up one of the glasses and held it out while Francis poured a measure of brandy into it. The amber liquid seemed to glow in the exquisite goblet, catching the firelight as Alec swirled it around.

"To the future," he said.

Three sets of eyes turned on him, and he smiled at each of the men who meant so much to him, each in his own unique way. He was about to take a sip from the glass when he heard a commotion outside, followed by an icy draft as the door was flung open.

"Captain Weston, how surprising to find you in my house," a familiar voice intoned. "Particularly as there is a warrant out for your arrest."

THE room seemed inordinately hot and stuffy and the bed too lumpy as Kit tossed restlessly from side to side, unable to get comfortable. He lay awake, listening to Alec's steady breathing and Robert's guttural snores, wondering how they could sleep so peacefully. His mind was racing, filled with the sharp words and brittle thrust and parry he'd witnessed between Alec and the unexpected visitor, whose presence had instantly shattered the joy of the evening.

Mrs. Alexander McEwen had marched into the dining room, trailing a rush of cold air in her wake, dispelling the happy mood with one icy glare of her beautiful green eyes. Kit had scrambled to his feet, hastily donning his doublet and pulling his clothing into some better semblance of order, noting out of the corner of his eye that both Robert and Alec were doing the same, albeit with less alarm. The evening had deteriorated after that, with Mrs. McEwen making no secret of her disdain for Alec, although Kit was unable to fathom what lay between them to cause such a reaction.

Jamie had done his best to conciliate, but Kit had felt the rising discomfort in the room, not least when Mrs. McEwen had turned her eyes on him, and with one withering glance had made him feel simultaneously inconsequential and like an unwelcome irritant. Alec had called a halt to the evening as soon as Mrs. McEwen's stern gaze had fallen on Kit, but not before Kit recognized the scorn and revulsion that told him how deeply she disapproved of him, though she could surely not have known who he was or what he'd done.

Kit slipped out of bed quietly and crossed the floor, the rough rush matting tickling his bare feet. Tipping his head, he stared up at the bright night sky and tried to erase the memory of that awful, knowing look. He'd seen it countless times before in the sneering faces of Marcus de Crecy's men, those swaggering braggarts who were envious of his closeness to Marcus while despising what he had to do to maintain the man's mercurial favor; he'd seen it in the carefully modulated derision of innkeepers and tavern owners who didn't have the courage to chastise Marcus for his public displays of affection toward Kit, but who had no qualms about voicing their disgust when Kit was alone. And though he'd tried to bury the memory, he thought he'd caught a fleeting glimpse of that same distaste on his mother's face when she had first set eyes on him outside the church in Stretton.

A noise beside him made him turn to find that Alec was out of bed and had crept up beside him. He wore only woolen drawers, his naked chest bared to the pale moonlight shining through the narrow window. In the silver glow, the whip marks on Alec's body were more noticeable, and Kit felt his own lacerations throb in sympathy. Although he'd felt the sting of Marcus's wrath a number of times, it still surprised him that Alec had been treated that way; the League was brutal in its dealings, but it rarely toyed with anybody it wanted dead, preferring instant dispatch that sent a clear message.

"Couldn't sleep?" Alec asked.

Kit shrugged. He hadn't planned on pressing Alec, but the words slipped out of his mouth. "Why does Jamie's mother dislike you so?" He almost regretted the question when a shadow passed over Alec's face. Alec remained silent for a moment, then fetched up a deep sigh.

"It's cold," he said. "If you are to have this story, we'd be better off under the covers."

He turned and led the way back to his bed, and Kit followed, curious to hear the tale, yet dreading anything that would intensify the hurt on Alec's face. They both climbed up onto the high bed, facing each other, and as Kit burrowed under the covers, Alec twitched a blanket over his own shoulders and huddled into its warmth. In the adjacent bed, Robert shuffled and sighed gustily before settling down again, his soft snores the only sound in the otherwise silent room. Alec glanced away, and it looked as though he was gathering his thoughts.

"My mother died when I was born," he began quietly. "My father and Jamie's had been business partners and friends, so when my father died of a fever some years later, Alexander McEwen took me in. Jamie and I grew up together in this house." He smiled softly, as though recalling fond memories. "I loved him from the start," he continued, the smile now tinged with sadness. "He was then as you find him now, filled with wonder and endlessly curious, passionate and patient in equal measures. We planned to travel the world on his father's fleet." Alec fell silent again, his eyes growing distant.

"Did his mother dislike you even then?" Kit prompted.

Alec shook his head. "She never had the warmth of Jamie's father, he was a singular man, but she seemed to care well enough for me."

"What happened to change that?" Kit asked.

Alec bit his lip, and Kit could see that the painful memories were welling up. "As time passed, Jamie and I grew even closer; we were rarely ever apart. But she thought my feelings for Jamie were too wild and uncontrolled, too *unnatural*." The emphasis he put on the word led Kit to believe that it was the exact term she had used. He could conjure up the scene in his mind: Alec bewildered by her accusatory manner, chastened by the insinuation in her voice; Mrs. McEwen, overbearing and judgmental, turning those cold green eyes on the young man who had never thought to disguise his feelings.

"She made her disapproval plain. She said some things…." He trailed off, shrugging the unspoken words away, as though too disturbed to share them. "After that I pulled away from Jamie," he continued. "I joined the City Guard and moved out of this house. I tried to see him as no more than a brother. I could tell he was hurt, but he let me pretend, and soon we spent more time avoiding each other than being together."

"And you?" Kit asked, watching as the light faded from Alec's eyes.

"I still loved him," Alec murmured. "But I learned to hide it, especially around his mother. One adapts when one is young." He lapsed into silence again, and Kit's heart hurt for him, for both young men forced to feign indifference when all they felt was love.

"But if you broke with Jamie, why does his mother still disapprove?" Kit asked.

Alec frowned. "I stayed away as much as possible. I had my duties with the Guard to keep me occupied, and Jamie had started to travel. But when his father fell ill, I came more frequently to the house to visit. At the end—" He stopped suddenly, then swallowed hard. "Jamie and I became close again over those last weeks. I cared deeply for Alexander, and shared grief overcomes most barriers. We were both in the room when his father finally passed, and I was comforting him when his mother walked in. She became hysterical when she saw him in my arms. She accused me of depravity and deceit, she even blamed me for Alexander's death, though he had been ailing for months and had always looked kindly on me. In the end, her constant railing wore me down. I accepted a posting to Shrewsbury. I left three years ago and have not returned until now." The last sentences had tumbled out of him as though a wall had broken, but he was quiet now, all words exhausted.

Kit reached out and laid a hand on Alec's arm, and Alec shook himself and smiled wanly. "Alexander was a kind man," he said. "He left me a generous bequest. I was able to purchase a house and live a little better than a captain in the City Guard usually does."

"And now you're selling your house," Kit said.

Alec's smile broadened. "What need do I have of a house while I'm sailing the seven seas?"

Kit felt his heart thud against his chest. "You really mean to take to the seas?" he asked.

"If it's what you want," Alec replied.

Kit squeezed Alec's arm tightly. "With all my heart," he murmured, the decision suddenly as clear and sharp as Jamie's Venetian crystal.

"Then we shall do so together," Alec said. The faraway look returned to his face, sadness settling in again. "It seems as though I was destined to sail the McEwen fleet," he said softly. "I just presumed that Jamie would be by my side when I did."

WHEN Kit woke, the bed was empty and Alec's clothes were gone. Kit presumed that he had left early in order to conclude his business with Jamie.

"He protects her even now."

Robert's voice made Kit jump. He turned toward the other bed to find Robert sitting on its edge, running his hand through his close-cropped hair.

"Protects who?" Kit asked.

Robert gestured with his head toward the half-open door. "That she-wolf who gave birth to Jamie," he said bluntly.

Kit realized that Robert must have been awake during the night, listening to Alec's tale. "You know the story?" he asked.

"Aye. I've had it from Alec and Jamie, though neither knows it. She didn't just tell Alec that his feelings were *unnatural*, she called him some pretty filthy names too. And that wasn't the worst of it."

"What else did she say?" Kit asked, dreading anything that might be worse than he'd already heard.

Robert shot him a sidelong glance. "She told Alec that Jamie knew of the unnatural feelings and was sickened by them," he said. "She told him though Jamie was disgusted he was too compassionate to show it. She really knew how to twist the knife." He shook his head and frowned. "When she saw them together after her husband died, I imagine she feared they would find their way back to each other and discover her poisoned lies. She made life exceedingly difficult for Alec, and when she started making ugly threats, he left."

"He didn't consider Jamie's feelings?" Kit asked. It seemed at odds with what he knew about Alec that he could give up so easily.

"That was all he considered," Robert said sharply. "He wouldn't see Jamie caught in the middle, so he didn't expose her deceit or her endless scheming. He told Jamie only that he and Mrs. McEwen had argued and that he felt he had to leave. So he went without revealing what a manipulative viper that woman is, and all to spare Jamie's feelings."

Any relief that Kit felt faded instantly as the sadness of the situation sank in. Alec's desire to protect Jamie from the harsh truth about his mother had destroyed any chance of fulfilling their dreams together and left both men bereft. A sudden thought struck. "It must be so painful for Alec to come back here," he said. Robert refrained from agreeing, but the look on his face told its own story. "But he did it to help me," Kit whispered.

Robert shrugged. "That, my friend, is Alec Weston," he said simply.

CHAPTER 6

DAWN had scarcely begun to illuminate the great square keep of Ludlow Castle, and at that hour there were few people abroad, but as Alec hurried along the narrow streets, he kept the collar of his cloak pulled high in order to obscure his face. Too many people knew him here, and temptation in the form of a price on his head had already been put in their way; he saw no reason to goad the fates by being reckless.

Despite the early hour, Jamie had already left the house by the time Alec arose. He'd left a message with Francis that Alec was to meet him at the Old Angel on Broad Street in order to finalize the sale of his house and chattels. Alec didn't consider himself a sentimental man, but he felt a twinge of regret that the property he'd purchased with Alexander McEwen's bequest would soon be lost, and with it his last tie to the man. He had loved Alexander dearly and had felt as bereft at his death as at the passing of his own father.

Jamie greeted him warmly at the old coaching inn and escorted him up a dark flight of stairs. "I thought it best not to take any chances," he muttered, opening a door into a small back room. A table was set up in the middle of the room, a lamp on it burning brightly, and behind the desk sat a man Alec recognized as Alexander's notary—Jamie's now, he assumed.

"You remember Thomas Marchant?" Jamie asked.

"Indeed I do," Alec replied. "How are you?" He shook the hand Thomas held out to him, not surprised when his question met with only a perfunctory nod. Thomas had always been an odd fellow, prone to keeping his own counsel, which probably served him well in his line of work. Although Alec had met him on many occasions, he doubted he had heard Thomas utter more than ten words that were not directly tied to some business transaction or the other.

"Sit," Jamie said, waving Alec into the only other chair in the room, directly opposite Thomas.

"I've drawn up the papers as you requested, sir," Thomas said, glancing up at Jamie.

"You found a buyer already?" Alec asked, halfway between gratitude and gloom.

Jamie smiled faintly. "It is what you wanted, isn't it?"

Alec shook himself, wondering at this sudden mawkishness. "Yes, of course," he said quickly. He turned back toward Thomas and asked, "What do I need to know?"

Thomas flicked through a stack of documents, pulled one out and turned it to face Alec. "Just sign here, sir, and all will be settled."

Alec took up a quill and dipped it into the inkwell beside the sheaf of papers. He read quickly through the document, then stopped and stared up into Jamie's face. "I don't understand," he said, frowning.

Jamie shrugged. "It's simple enough," he replied. "I'll rent the house for a period of one year. I'm advancing you the whole of the annual amount. When you return from your travels, the house will be yours again."

Alec pointed at the parchment. "This sum is far too great for one year of rent," he said. "Besides, what do you need with a house in Shrewsbury?"

Jamie raised an eyebrow, a gesture reminiscent of his father. "I believe it is customary for the renter to complain about the high rate, not the other way around," he said crisply. "As for what I'll do with the house, that, my old friend, is my business." He leaned down until his face was level with Alec's. "I want to do this, Alec," he said, his tone softening. "Take the trip, give yourself some time to think things through. If you still want to sell in a year's time, we'll find a real buyer and get you the price you deserve."

Gratitude welled up in Alec; he looked away from Jamie's sincere gaze and fixed his eyes on the document in front of him, his hand trembling slightly as he signed his name. "Thank you," he murmured. There were so many things he wanted to say, but for the moment those were the only words that mattered. Jamie patted him briefly on the back, then signaled to Thomas, who gathered up his documents and stacked them neatly.

"I'll have a letter of credit drawn up," Thomas said. "You'll be able to obtain funds wherever you travel." Alec looked up into Thomas's face, unsure how much the man knew about Alec's plan to take to the seas and disappear from these shores until things cooled off. Thomas returned his gaze, but there seemed nothing more than mild curiosity behind his impassive stare.

"Very well," Alec said, turning back to Jamie. "The house is yours for a year. We'll discuss its future when I'm a little more assured of my own. To that end"—he nodded toward Thomas—"I'd like another document drawn up. Should I fail to return for whatever reason...." He held up a hand to forestall Jamie's protests. "Should I fail to return to Ludlow within a year, whatever the reason," he repeated distinctly, "then the house and all its contents will be yours. It's the only way I'll accept this offer."

It was easy to read the train of thoughts that crossed Jamie's mind, reflected as they were on his expressive face. In the end, he simply nodded.

"I'll draw up a separate agreement," Thomas said politely. He rose and gathered his things together.

"Will you join us for breakfast?" Jamie asked.

Thomas shook his head. "Thank you, but no. I have work to do," he said shortly. He nodded briskly to Alec and walked out of the room.

"I'll have breakfast served up here," Jamie said. "Give me a moment?"

He followed Thomas out, and Alec listened as they both clattered down the wooden staircase. He crossed to the small window that overlooked Broad Street, and watched idly as Thomas departed the inn and hurried away. He wondered briefly why Jamie had asked to meet the notary here rather than have him come to the house as was customary, realizing with a start that Jamie must be anxious to hide this business transaction if he was willing to risk Alec being recognized in the streets of Ludlow.

He turned as the door reopened and Jamie came back in. "Food is on its way," he said. He waved Alec back into his chair and sat opposite him, looking satisfied with his morning's work.

"Your mother was none too pleased to see us last night," Alec observed, guessing that she was the one Jamie was trying to avoid.

Jamie winced. "I'm sorry, I thought she had thawed toward you."

"It doesn't appear so," Alec said dryly.

"She was genuinely concerned when you were taken by the League," Jamie protested mildly. "She sent every day to the barracks for word of you."

Alec thought it more likely that she had simply put on a good face in front of her son, though it was possible that she had felt some small remorse at the shabby way she had treated Alec when her husband died. "Does she know anything about our discussions here?" he asked.

"She doesn't concern herself with business," Jamie said quickly.

"And you won't be telling her, I'll warrant," Alec remarked.

"This is between us, Alec," Jamie said, his green eyes finding Alec's own and holding fast. "Are you decided, then? Will you take me up on the offer of a passage to Bruges?"

Alec smiled. "Kit likes the idea," he said. "Even Robert seemed interested. I think it possible you'll make seamen of us yet."

"I wish I could come with you," Jamie said wistfully. "You remember the plans we made when we were young? We were going to find new lands, new trade routes. We were going to rule the waves together."

"Aye, and never put down roots, just live the life of the sea, going where the currents swept us. Such a beautiful, foolish dream." He hadn't meant to sound so harsh, but he could tell by the hurt on Jamie's face that his bitterness had seeped through. "Did you ever consider traveling more?" he asked, trying to take some of the sting off.

Jamie shook his head vigorously. "As you say, just childish dreams," he said, though the longing in his voice belied the brisk words. He shrugged. "When my father died, I had to take over running the business. I fear my sailing days are far behind me."

Alec's heart swelled with pity. With Kit he felt he had the chance to recapture some of the boundless possibilities that had fueled his youth, but for Jamie it seemed as though those hopes and dreams were fading; his life now bound by duty and obligation, and constrained by the world's narrow expectations.

A boy appeared beside the table and deposited two brimming mugs of ale, swiftly followed by plates of mutton and cabbage. The food was hearty, though it couldn't compare to the delicious tastes that were commonplace at Jamie's own table. They ate in silence for a few moments, Alec studying Jamie's face, seeing for the first time the lines that crinkled his eyes and tugged at the corners of his mouth. He looked so much like his father, despite having his mother's coloring and features.

"It isn't too late, you know," he said quietly.

Jamie quirked a quizzical eyebrow. "Too late for what?" he asked.

"To live the life you always wanted," Alec said. "To find somebody to share your dreams with."

Jamie turned his beautiful green eyes on Alec and smiled sadly. "I've never felt for anybody what I feel for you. I don't expect I ever will."

Alec felt a pang of loss for all that might have been. When Alexander died, they had come so close to rekindling what had been between them, until Mrs. McEwen's scheming had once more driven them apart. For one bright moment, he saw the life they could have had: constant travel far and wide, the collection of curios in the house growing steadily with each passing year, the love between them deepening over time. They could have been happy together, he was sure of it.

When he looked back across the table, he noticed that Jamie's small smile was at odds with the desolation in his eyes. "I've accepted what my life has become, and what it can never be," Jamie said. "It's up to you now to make our dreams come alive."

THOUGH her husband had died some three years ago, Mrs. Alexander McEwen still wore widow's black every day, eschewing all adornment with the exception of a heavy silver crucifix that hung around her neck. She was a handsome woman, with thick black hair shot through with gray but still lustrous, and remarkably unlined skin that made her look younger than her actual years. Her green eyes were striking, although steely, and her lips were sensual and full, though too often thinned with displeasure. She sat now in the formal parlor of her house, her eyes focused on Kit, who was trying his best not to squirm under her coolly appraising gaze.

"My son tells me you will be leaving Ludlow soon," she said, the words clipped and precise. It was the first time she had spoken directly to Kit, and he was not surprised to find that she was eager to see the back of him.

"Yes, ma'am," he replied, not really sure what to call her. Alec had been very formal last night, addressing her only as "Mrs. McEwen," and she had returned the protocol, never using his first name, only his former title.

"You will be returning to your home, I assume?" she asked.

"I'm afraid that isn't an option," Kit said.

"No, of course not," she sniffed. "I doubt your family would welcome a lawbreaker back into the fold."

Kit flushed hotly at the rebuke but held his tongue. In truth she scared him a little with her imperious manner and an aversion toward him that was all too apparent. There was a prolonged pause while Mrs. McEwen gave him a sober, searching look, and Kit tried his hardest not to fidget.

"And where will you be going when you leave here?" she eventually inquired.

"I believe Captain Weston is discussing that with your son," Kit answered carefully.

"What has my son got to do with this?" Mrs. McEwen snapped.

Kit bit his lip, not sure how much to tell her about the plan they were formulating. Her eyes bored into him, and she tapped impatiently on the arm of her chair, clearly waiting for an answer.

"I believe Jamie has some information that Alec thinks might be useful…" He trailed off as her expression hardened, aware he had said something to displease her, though not sure what.

"He shows up here after a three-year absence, trailing a criminal in his wake, bringing God knows what kind of danger to my doorstep," she hissed. "What does he expect us to do for him?"

Though stung by her cruelty, Kit kept a tight rein on his emotions. "Alec turned to Jamie as a friend," he said, as steadily as he could.

"A friend who can provide money, no doubt," she sneered. "How dare he use my son to help him escape justice—"

"Whose justice, madam?"

Kit wasn't sure he'd ever been more grateful to hear Robert's dispassionate voice. He turned his head to find his friend standing in the doorway, watching Mrs. McEwen with an unreadable expression on his face.

"The Lord Chancellor himself has issued a warrant against you," she said.

"Arlen is a double-dealing snake," Robert said flatly. "He used us to trap the boy and lead him into harm."

"He ordered you to do your job," Mrs. McEwen countered. "Arresting a member of the most notorious gang of thieves in the kingdom is what you are paid for, is it not?"

"He was coerced into that gang, as Arlen knew very well."

"How so? He stayed with the League for three years, to hear my son tell it."

Kit knew he was blushing fiercely to be discussed so freely, as though his presence was irrelevant. He wanted to tell them both to stop, but he was unable to open his mouth, let alone form the words. Robert glanced over and caught his eye, and seemed to suddenly realize that he was trespassing on Kit's feelings. He drew in a sharp breath and let it out with a sigh.

"Madam, you would not wish to know the answer to your question. I'm sure your son thought to spare you the details. But do not presume to pass judgment." He turned away, ignoring the anger that made her face flush red. "Kit, I could use your help," he said abruptly, lifting his chin to indicate the door.

Kit scrambled gratefully to his feet and gave Mrs. McEwen a small bow. She was practically vibrating with suppressed fury, and Kit could scarcely move quickly enough to escape her. He followed Robert out into the hallway, closed the door quietly behind him, and breathed out a great sigh of relief.

Robert rounded on him, wagging a warning finger. "You'd do well, my lad, not to say anything to that woman," he said curtly.

"I can't just ignore her," Kit protested. "She asked me a question."

"Well, stay out of her way, then," Robert ordered. "We have enough to contend with without aggravating her. She isn't exactly well-disposed toward the captain to begin with."

Kit thought it singularly unfair of Robert to hold him to blame simply for trying to be polite, but he was too glad to have been rescued from her interrogation to hold a grudge. Instead he hurried after Robert, stopping only when they reached the stout wooden door. "Are we going out?" he asked, hopefully.

"You're to have a sword," Robert replied. "I suppose you know how to use one?" he added doubtfully.

"I spent three years with the Sun League," Kit huffed, allowing a little sarcasm to color his tone. "Marcus trained me himself."

He looked away from Robert's penetrating gaze, trying to control the dread that he thought must be evident on his face. *I'll not have a useless fop hanging off my coattails,* Marcus had sneered. Kit could still hear the cruel laughter of Marcus's men as they witnessed his struggle to learn the weapon to their leader's satisfaction, though thankfully they soon became bored of Marcus's relentless drills and endless practice sessions and eventually left him alone. In the end, Kit was as proficient with the sword as any one of the jeering watchers, though he'd never been allowed to actually wear a weapon in Marcus's presence.

If Robert guessed at the discomfort the memories dredged up, he was considerate enough not to show it. "Come then," he said gruffly. "Keep your head down and stay close. Jamie has a man who will see you right."

"HOW dare you involve my family in your treason!"

Alec had scarcely crossed the threshold into the study when Jamie's mother pushed the door open and started to berate him.

"It isn't bad enough that you drag that criminal into my house, now you compound your disregard for decency by involving my son in your escape attempt," she fumed.

Alec drew in a calming breath, determined not to allow this to descend into an argument. "Jamie is helping us out of the goodness of his heart," he began, but she waved his words away as though swatting a troublesome fly.

"He's doing this because of you," she spat. "You always knew how to take advantage of his good nature."

Despite his silent admonition to avoid being baited by her, Alec felt a hot splash of anger rise up. Inevitably, he recalled the last time he had spoken to her, after her husband's death, and the bitter accusations she'd flung in his face, along with her threat to expose him for immorality and her claim that he had corrupted Jamie and led him into sin. Years before, she had forced him to doubt himself, had twisted what he felt into something base and degrading and convinced him that his feelings for Jamie were unwelcome. When Alexander had died and Alec had held Jamie in his arms, he'd realized that everything she'd told him had been a lie. Jamie's love for him was so clear and strong, evident in the look in his eyes and in every gesture and word. But by the time Alec discovered the falsehood, it was too late. He couldn't undo the damage she had caused without exposing her appalling deceit, and he couldn't bear to see Jamie devastated by the ugly truth.

Still, he was no longer a boy to be intimidated by her, especially when there was so much at stake.

"Jamie knows his own mind on the matter," he said coolly.

"He knows only what you have told him," she scoffed. "How are we to know that you speak true?"

"Do you really think so ill of me?" Alec asked. At this point he wasn't sure that he cared anything for her opinion of him, but he doubted very much that Jamie had told her the whole story, and it irked him that her mind was made up without knowing the facts. She was very far from her son in that respect.

"I will do everything in my power to safeguard Jamie," he said stiffly. "But I have a duty to protect those I travel with."

Her lovely face became pinched and flushed. "How you choose to behave with that catamite is your business," she hissed. "But I will not allow you to drag my son into the mire with you."

Alec flinched at the heartless words. He drew himself up to full height and took a step forward, forcing her to tilt her head to look him in the eye. "Whatever distaste you feel toward me, that young man does not deserve your condemnation," he said, unable to keep the anger from his voice. "He is the innocent victim in this whole affair, and I'll be damned if I'll allow you to pass judgment on him."

The flush on her cheeks deepened to a dark red, and fury made her cold green eyes flash. "I wish my son had never laid eyes on you," she said. "Your perverted influence has robbed him of any hope of happiness."

The anger that had heated Alec's blood suddenly cooled, and he looked at the woman who had been the closest thing he had to a mother and felt nothing but pity for her. "Jamie could be happy yet," he said quietly, "if only you would let him find his own way."

Her eyes narrowed and her mouth thinned into a cruel line. "I'd rather see him dead," she said with such conviction that Alec knew she must have considered this alternative before. He wasn't fool enough to try to persuade her that she didn't mean it.

"I want you to get out of my house," she spat. "And take that degenerate outlaw with you—"

"It's my house, Mother, and they are welcome to stay as long as they want."

Alec spun around to find Jamie standing in the open doorway. He didn't know how long Jamie had been there or how much he had heard, but from the wounded expression on his face, it appeared he had witnessed more than he should. Mrs. McEwen's face turned ashen as she, too, realized what had been overheard.

"James, I…."

Jamie held up his hand. "There will be no argument," he said firmly. "I let Alec down once before at your insistence. I've regretted it ever since. I won't make the same mistake again."

Mrs. McEwen gathered herself up and swept out of the room, but not before shooting a poisonous look at Alec that chilled him to the bone.

"We should leave, Jamie," he said. "I don't wish to make trouble for you."

A frown creased Jamie's forehead. "First we'll conclude our business to your satisfaction, then we'll discuss the details of your voyage and make ready. Only then will you even think about leaving," he said resolutely.

Alec knew better than to argue. "We'll stay out of your way as much as possible," he said.

"You are my guest," Jamie said, articulating each word slowly. "If my mother doesn't like it, she is free to leave this house."

Alec threw up his hands in surrender, but he was unable to feel any sense of triumph. It was clear that his presence here was unwelcome, and that sheltering Kit only exacerbated the animosity that Mrs. McEwen already felt toward him. He had found himself on her wrong side too many times; he didn't think that she would concede without a struggle.

KIT would have liked to tarry for a few moments as they skirted the hill leading up to Ludlow Castle, but when he turned to look up at the gray stone wall, Robert reached for a handful of his cloak and yanked him forward, muttering a curse under his breath and sarcastically pointing out that this was not a Sunday outing.

Picking up the pace, Kit hurried after Robert and fell back into step beside him, remembering to hide his face when Robert cuffed him, none too gently, on the back of the head. "How you survived three years with the Sun League is a mystery," Robert grumbled.

Kit decided to ignore the jibe. "Have you ever been on a ship?" he asked instead.

"Aye," Robert answered shortly. Kit waited, but Robert seemed disinclined to elaborate.

"When?" he prodded patiently.

Robert scowled. "I wasn't born into the City Guard, you know," he said. "My life began up there." He jerked his head, and it took Kit a moment to realize that he had indicated the castle.

"You were Mortimer's man?" Kit asked, unable to hide his surprise.

"Right up until he swung at Tyburn," Robert replied grimly.

Kit waited for further information, but again Robert allowed silence to fall. Kit knew the story anyway; everybody in the shire still felt the taint of Roger Mortimer's scandalous betrayal and murder of the second King Edward. Kit had presumed that everybody who supported Mortimer had been cruelly dealt with; certainly the man himself had been found guilty, though without benefit of a fair trial, and had been executed in the chill of a November morning in the village of Tyburn.

"I was a lad when I entered his service," Robert said quietly. "I don't have to tell you that in this life it's a rare thing to get to choose your master or your fate."

Kit nodded in agreement.

"The new king isn't as vindictive as some," Robert continued, so softly that Kit had to strain to hear him. "He didn't blame the men for their master's folly. Mortimer's good lady wife was not so understanding. After his death, she dismissed all of his retainers, even though we'd had no option but to follow him, so I found a position with the Guard."

"You went overseas with Mortimer?" Kit asked, not certain how far to intrude into Robert's private affairs. But surprisingly Robert didn't seem to mind the questions.

"Aye. When I was a lad not much older than you, I accompanied him to France."

"After he escaped from the Tower?" Kit breathed, undisguised awe in his voice. It was a colorful tale that had passed down through the years, doubtless growing in daring and intrigue as it traveled. Kit had heard it a dozen times, but never from somebody who might actually know the truth of it.

Robert shot him a sour look. "Before you ask, it wasn't like in the ballads, boy," he growled. "We rotted in exile in France for three miserable years while he plotted against his own king, then when we returned home, we all got caught up in his treason." He turned his head away and spat. "We are all of us just game pieces in the affairs of our betters, to be moved around as they see fit."

The darkness in his tone made Kit wonder what Robert had seen or done to make him seem so bitter. It was easy enough to guess; Robert would have had plenty of opportunities to see the very worst of humanity under Mortimer's command. Adultery, treachery, betrayal, even murder: Mortimer's greedy ambition had encompassed them all. It made Robert's dedication to Alec—a moral man worthy of loyalty and absolute trust—wholly understandable.

Kit was about to press for more details about life in service to Roger Mortimer when Robert hissed out a curse, spun around, and slammed Kit up against a wall, turning his own back to the street.

"Christ's blood," Kit exclaimed, momentarily winded.

"Quiet," Robert ordered, pushing Kit back roughly when he tried to step forward. "Do you see the two Guards on the corner?"

Kit brushed Robert's hand off his chest, but he peered over Robert's shoulder and saw two City Guardsmen walking toward them. "Aye," he murmured.

"I shared barracks with them for a year," Robert said. "If they see me, they'll know Alec is near, and we'll be lost."

A shiver of dread tingled down Kit's spine. The two Guards were getting closer, and one had noticed them and was looking at them curiously. The Guards might simply pass them by, but Kit knew they couldn't take that chance. "Go as soon as I move," he whispered. "Wait for me at the end of the street."

Robert's hand shot out again, trying to hold him fast, but Kit shook him off and crossed the street, noting how the Guards tensed at his approach, their hands falling to rest on the hilt of their swords. Out of the corner of his eye, he saw Robert slip away, pulling his cloak about him as though suddenly chilled, effectively shielding his face from detection.

"Excuse me, gentlemen," Kit said loudly, pulling both pairs of eyes toward him as Robert hurried away.

"What is it?" one of the Guards asked.

"I'm a newcomer to Ludlow, sir," Kit said, giving one of his most innocent looks. "Would you be able to tell me how to find Old Street?"

One of the men looked him up and down contemptuously. "Do we look as though we have time to waste giving directions to lost children?" he sneered. The second Guard's eyes had returned to Robert's retreating back, and they were narrowing now, squinting against the harsh sunlight.

"You look like men who know where to find the liveliest brothel," Kit said quickly, gratified when the other Guard's startled eyes snapped back to his face.

The man who had spoken tugged at his sword, unsheathing one third of it with a hiss and glint of steel. "Be off with you before I decide to teach you some manners, boy," he snarled.

"Of course, sir," Kit said with a small bow. "I must have the wrong information." He turned on his heel and walked away, but not before seeing the ghost of a grin flickering across the faces of both men.

He knew enough to keep his pace steady, despite the fact that he itched to take to his heels and run. When he reached the end of the street, he heard a low whistle and swung to his right into a narrow lane. Robert was standing in the shadow of a porch, and Kit hurried over to him, watching Robert's eyes as they scoured the road behind his back. Obviously happy with what he saw, Robert relaxed noticeably, though a frown darkened his expression.

"Do you know what Alec would have done if I'd returned home without you?" he growled.

"And what he'd have done if I'd let you get taken?" Kit countered.

"That was damned reckless—" Robert started.

"It was a calculated risk," Kit cut in firmly. "I've played decoy dozens of times before. We had no other choice." He tensed, waiting for Robert to continue to rail against him, but the man only mumbled an oath and then grimaced.

"Best keep this little incident to ourselves," he suggested, arching an eyebrow. "I doubt either of us will escape a lecture if Alec finds out."

"Agreed," Kit said, none too keen to face Alec's reproof. He fell into step once more as Robert hurried down the street and away from the Guards. Kit shot him a sidelong glance. "Do you see now how I survived the League?" he asked.

Robert's expression didn't change, but he made a sound like a strangled laugh. "I'm willing to concede you have your uses," he said dryly.

THE beautiful hand-drawn map that Jamie spread across his desk was covered in a dozen tiny lines, each representing a different trade route from England to Europe.

"Here," he said, his finger sweeping across the parchment. "This is the route you'll take."

They all crowded around and bent their heads closer, following the path Jamie outlined. They would first have to travel overland to the port of Boston in Lincolnshire, then take one of Jamie's merchant vessels across the channel to the Flemish port of Bruges. From there, smaller vessels would load up the ship's cargo of wool and finished cloth and transport it through the extensive canal system to various towns throughout the region. It all seemed so thrilling to Kit, although he noticed that the others were not nearly as excited by the prospect of the journey.

"You'll have letters of introduction to the captain of the *Alexander McEwen*," Jamie said, and Kit felt an additional burst of exhilaration to know they would be traveling on Jamie's flagship. "It will be safer if you travel to Boston ahead of the wool shipment," Jamie continued. "You'll be slowed down otherwise. You can lodge at the White Hart Inn while you wait for the goods to arrive and be loaded. The innkeeper knows me and will look out for you."

"When is she scheduled to set sail?" Alec asked.

Jamie opened his ledger and ran his finger down a neatly inscribed column of figures. "We have two ships sailing this month," he murmured, scanning the page closely. "The *Alexander McEwen* weighs anchor ten days hence." He glanced around and smiled ruefully. "I'm afraid she won't be able to wait for you. There's a rumor that King Edward intends to forbid the export of wool to Flanders—this might be the last shipment we get out for many months. If you don't arrive in time, she'll have to cast off without you."

"Understood," Alec said. He scratched his chin as he studied the map carefully. "And the best road to Boston, you think?"

Jamie shook his head. "I think it might be better if nobody knows the exact route you plan to take," he said, looking directly into Alec's eyes. Something passed between them that Kit couldn't read, but Alec simply nodded and murmured his assent.

"And once we reach Bruges?" he asked.

Jamie shrugged. "The choice will be yours," he said. "You can follow the shipment farther inland, or you can wait while the return goods are loaded. We'll be bringing back furs coming in from the Baltic. It will likely take a week or two to arrange. You are most welcome to make the return voyage if you think it will be safe enough to come home."

Alec exchanged a look with Robert. "I think we might wait to make that decision," he said.

Jamie nodded his agreement. "The sea voyage will take two weeks. You'll be traveling under the guise of wool traders." He paused for a moment, and his eyes fell on Kit. "I'm afraid you might have to act the part of the servant," he said apologetically.

Kit was sure that he heard Robert snort in amusement, but when he looked over, his friend's features were well schooled to innocence. "Gladly," he said, scowling at Robert.

"Thomas will have the final documents drawn up by this evening," Jamie continued. "All that remains after that is to pack your bags and saddle your mounts."

Alec raised his head from the map. "We can't thank you enough, Jamie," he said sincerely. "I'm not sure what we'd have done without your help."

"No doubt you'd have come up with some wild scheme or another," Jamie laughed.

"Nothing as ideal as this," Robert said. "It gets us out of the way of two very powerful and equally vengeful forces. We can wait in safety until this blows itself out and all is forgotten."

"And if worse comes to worse, we can start a new life overseas," Alec added.

"Alec is right," Robert said. "There is no way we can thank you."

"It's what friends do for each other," Jamie dismissed. "I'm sure were the circumstances different, I could count on you in the same way." His cheeks were flushed red, and Kit felt that he was trying to cover his discomfiture when he turned and said, "Did my man help you find a suitable weapon?"

"Yes, he did, thank you," Kit said, exchanging a quick glance with Robert.

"And you encountered no difficulties on the way?" Alec asked with some suspicion in his voice.

Robert shrugged. "We looked out for each other, Captain," he said, neatly managing to avoid a lie.

That evening Kit found himself seated opposite Alec in the long dining room, listening as he and Jamie exchanged fond memories of their shared past. Robert had slipped out earlier in the afternoon, with a promise to rejoin them before sunrise the next day. Alec had murmured something into his friend's ear that brought a smile to his face, and had let him go without protest, though it was clear from Alec's tense expression that he was worried.

"He'll be fine," Jamie reassured. "He knows the place inside and out. He can easily avoid those he doesn't want to see."

Kit thought back to their encounter with the City Guards and felt his own tension ratchet up, but he trusted in Robert's competence and skill.

Mrs. McEwen had excused herself from dinner, pleading a headache. Jamie and Alec had accepted her excuse with the proper solicitous words, but both seemed as relieved as Kit that she wouldn't be joining them on this their last evening together.

The room echoed with laughter as Jamie and Alec recounted stories, each following seamlessly from the other as though well rehearsed, even though Kit knew that they hadn't spoken in three years. They looked so happy together; it was easy to see in them the young boys they had once been, making endless plans and devoted to each other in all things.

"What say you, Kit?"

Kit hadn't been following the conversation closely and started at Alec's question. "I'm sorry," he mumbled, flushing with embarrassment at having been caught out.

Alec just grinned at him. "Don't apologize," he said. "It must be very dull for you listening to all our old stories."

"Not at all," Kit hurried out. "I love finding out what you were like back then." It was true; until his mind had wandered, he had heard wonderful tales of Alec's youth, before Mrs. McEwen's bitter acrimony had spoiled the perfection of those earlier days.

"What about you, Kit?" Jamie asked kindly. "What were your younger years like?"

Kit shrugged, casting back to the time before Marcus de Crecy had changed his life so irrevocably, but it was difficult to recall much. He had trained himself to let go of those memories, to erase his family from his mind; it was hard now to conjure up those happier, simpler times. Jamie sensed his struggle and put a hand on his arm, squeezing briefly.

"You'll be able to create a different life now," he said gently, his green eyes filled with compassion. "New memories that will last a lifetime."

Kit nodded, grateful for Jamie's understanding. He glanced across the table and into Alec's face, and was warmed by the smile he found there. Jamie changed the subject quickly, and soon he and Alec were once more trading fond reminiscences. They looked so comfortable together that when Francis brought in a third bottle of wine, Kit rose.

"I'm going to go to bed," he said.

Alec started to stand, but Kit waved him back into his chair. "You two carry on," he said quickly. "You'll want to say your good-byes."

"Are you sure?" Alec asked.

"Of course," Kit replied. It was plain from the look on Alec's face that he needed more time with his old friend, and as Kit left the room after saying good night, Alec and Jamie were huddled close with heads bent, the low hum of their voices suggesting an intimacy that stirred unfamiliar envy in Kit.

He mounted the stairs slowly until he reached their large room, and after several moments of checking the few belongings in his travel pack, he undressed and climbed into bed. Moonlight threw shadows across the dark ceiling as Kit lay on his back, head resting on his laced hands, contemplating the path his life had taken to this point. It seemed impossible that having never set foot out of the shire, he was now on the verge of a journey that would take him overseas to a new country, perhaps a brand-new life. Even if he had allowed any dreams to penetrate the walls he had built around himself, he doubted he would have had the imagination to envision himself here.

Kit didn't know he had drifted off to sleep until a sound woke him from a light doze. When his eyes adjusted to the darkness, he realized that Alec was now in the room, standing in front of the narrow window, utterly still, his eyes turned heavenward. Kit rolled off the bed, hissing as his bare feet touched the cool floor. He padded across the room, the clean rushes crackling underfoot, and came to stand beside Alec, who looked at him and smiled faintly. Even in the dim light, it was easy to see the melancholy that darkened his expression.

"You said your good-byes?" Kit asked. "That must have been hard."

"Aye," Alec replied, turning his face to the moon once again.

Kit wanted to offer some comfort, but he wasn't used to being in this position and didn't know how to find the words. He wished Robert were here; for all his taciturn nature, he seemed to know how to provide a gruff kind of support when his captain needed it.

In the end, Alec broke the awkward silence himself. "I didn't expect it to be just as painful as the last time we parted," he said.

"I suppose you don't know when you'll see him again," Kit said. "Just like the last time."

Alec looked at him thoughtfully, then nodded. "I think you might be right," he agreed.

Kit looked closely at Alec's face, wondering if he dared ask the question that had crept into his mind over the past days. He finally decided that his friend would not take offense. "You love him still?" he ventured quietly.

Alec turned toward him. "I'll always love Jamie," he said, before falling into silence again. Kit watched a range of emotions chase each other across Alec's face, and he held his breath, unsure whether he wanted to hear anything more. For a brief moment, he wished that they had never set foot in Alec's childhood home and rekindled the hurts alongside the joys, but he swiftly banished that unworthy thought. If Alec's happiness lay with Jamie McEwen, they both deserved to know it.

"Perhaps you'd rather stay in Ludlow?" Kit offered, the words almost sticking in his throat. Although it would be a challenge, he felt sure that Alec could work things out with Anthony Arlen and the City Guard, maybe even return to his old life. Robert would likely be just as pleased to stay in the town that had once been his home instead of dragging himself across the sea to a foreign land. The air of adventure that had once characterized this journey suddenly vanished, leaving the reality of a hard road and, ultimately, exile.

Alec frowned as though having trouble understanding, then his brow smoothed and his eyes widened. "It isn't like that." He smiled grimly. "Jamie's mother would be pleased," he said, bitterness underlying his words. "I think of him more as a brother now. Anything else has become impossible for us."

Despite his best intentions, Kit felt relief well up in him. He was sad for the two young men whose hopes had been trampled into the dust, and the prospect of Jamie finding that kind of happiness again seemed bleak, but a fierce longing for Alec had taken hold, and Kit knew that it would be hard to let that go now.

He reached to cover Alec's cold hand with his own. "And you're still content to leave this life behind?" he asked.

Alec smiled. "Robert puts it best," he said. "The City Guard has become little more than an instrument for Anthony Arlen's obsessions. It was getting harder to live a life of honor. We're well out of it."

"But to leave your home behind...." He stilled as Alec squeezed his hand.

"I spent my whole childhood dreaming of travel," Alec said. "I can't think of two people I'd rather share that dream with now."

THEIR horses were already saddled and tethered to a hitching post when Alec stepped out of the house and into the cool morning air. The pale dawn light was only just beginning to brighten the sky to the east, and the street was mostly empty, but Alec still looked around carefully, peering into the shadowy recesses in search of anything unusual or out of place. Satisfied that everything was as it should be, he quickly checked all three mounts, turning as the door opened and Robert came out to join him.

Robert had crept back into their room in the small hours of the morning and had lain on his bed fully clothed, dozing for a few hours until they all rose. Alec glanced over and smiled at the satisfied look on his friend's face. "Good night?" he asked innocently.

Robert returned his look, completely unabashed. "As ever," he replied blandly.

Alec winked at his old friend but refrained from teasing. Robert had spent the evening keeping company with the women who plied their trade in one of the better of the bawdy houses that lined Old Street, and clearly he had enjoyed the experience.

When the door opened again, Alec caught a glimpse of Kit and Jamie embracing quickly before they, too, stepped out of the house. All four of them had shared a hasty breakfast in Jamie's study while he wrapped several documents in a cloth before handing them over to Alec. He also handed over a small amount of coin, the first installment of the rent he had offered on Alec's house. The rest would be collected along the way as needed, the amounts indicated in the letters of credit that Alec had tucked into his tunic.

The rushed meal had been a somber affair, each of them silently wondering what the future would bring, and whether, despite their optimistic assurances, they would ever see each other again.

Alec smiled a greeting as Jamie walked down the steps and joined him. They had said their private farewells the night before, Alec promising to return within a year to reclaim the title deeds to his house, and Jamie pledging his eternal friendship and swearing that as long as he lived, Alec would always have a home in Ludlow. By silent, mutual consent, neither had mentioned Jamie's mother or what she might think of the offer.

"All set?" Jamie asked, with a perfunctory tug on Alec's stirrups.

"As ready as we are likely to be," Alec replied.

"And you know the route you will take into Boston?" Alec nodded. "And you have all your travel papers and remember the name of the ship and her captain?" Jamie pressed.

Alec grinned at his friend. "Didn't you ask those same questions last night?"

Jamie shrugged. "And you'll take good care of yourselves?" he asked, his voice gentler, and tinged with anxiety.

"You don't imagine Robert will allow any harm to come to us, do you?" Alec replied lightly. He sobered up at the serious look on Jamie's face. "We'll all be fine," he said firmly. "I'll send word back once we reach Boston and make contact with your captain."

Jamie nodded and held out his hand, which Alec grasped tightly. "Take care, my old friend," Jamie said, looking deeply into Alec's eyes.

"And you," Alec replied. "I'll see you within a year, God willing."

Jamie smiled and released his hold, turning to shake hands quickly with Robert and Kit before standing back as all three of them mounted their horses.

Alec lifted his hand in salute as he took the lead, walking his horse slowly northward along the cobbled street. He couldn't resist turning to take a final look at the much-loved gray stone house and Jamie's grave but beautiful face. Out of the corner of his eye, he noticed a slight movement and caught a glimpse of a black-clad figure silhouetted in one of the upper casements. Raising his head, he locked eyes with Jamie's mother, startled at the intensity of her gaze and the look of hatred marring her lovely features. A sudden gust of wind sent a chill through him, and he pulled his thick cloak more tightly around his shoulders; when he looked back again, she had disappeared.

Despite the certainty that Mrs. McEwen despised him, Alec nonetheless felt a twinge of sorrow. Now that their fortunes were once more intertwined, he had nursed the foolish hope that she would thaw toward him and accept the fact that he was back in Jamie's life. After a final glance at the empty window, he turned his head away, glumly resigned to her enmity. Maybe she would never welcome him back into the family he had once loved so dearly, but there was nothing she could do to break his renewed bond with her son.

With that comforting thought, he led his small party toward the Gladford Gate and turned his mind to the next stage of their journey.

CHAPTER 7

As the great walls of Ludlow receded into the distance behind them, Alec felt a sudden, sharp burst of relief. Though they had not encountered any real trouble, he was glad to once more be traveling through open countryside, where it was easier to assess the possibility of danger.

Boston was some six days' easy ride away, and he and Robert had planned a direct route, though one that would keep them on the smaller back roads in order to avoid unwanted company. He set his mount to an easy trot, enjoying the warmth as the sun rose steadily and the bracing breeze that blew in from the west, cooling his face and tickling his nose with the pungent smell of grazing sheep and cattle.

Behind him he heard the low murmur of voices as Robert and Kit conversed, then a short burst of laughter. Alec smiled to himself; somewhere during the last few days, it seemed as though Kit had managed to impress Robert enough to gain his affection. Robert was not generally a man given to easy friendships, but his heart was big and his sense of justice was as sharp as a butcher's knife, and clearly he had been won over by Kit. Alec was glad of it; if Robert was going to abandon his livelihood and his home, then Alec would rather it was for something he believed in himself, and not simply because of his loyal support of Alec's decisions.

Robert's straightforward manner and rigorous guidance had been just what Alec had needed when he had fled the McEwen home all those years ago, smarting from the accusations that had been leveled at him, his heart in turmoil at the thought that Jamie was sickened by his attentions but too gracious to show it. Robert had taken him firmly in hand and taught him the basic lessons of discipline and command, resolutely shaping him until he was worthy of the captain's commission that Alexander McEwen's wealth made possible. Robert's respect and loyalty, once earned, had never been withdrawn, even when he had learned things about Alec that would likely have disgusted any other man.

The voices behind him continued intermittently, the only other sound besides the bleating of sheep and the whisper of wind through the branches overhead. It was much warmer now, and Alec was thankful that the canopy of trees offered substantial shade along the beaten path.

This was the road he had taken three years ago when he had left Ludlow for what he thought might be the last time, and it was hard not to let the tug of memory dispirit him. He had been overwhelmed with sorrow at Alexander's death, heartbroken at being parted from Jamie, and feeling friendless and alone after Mrs. McEwen's spiteful tirade and the threat of her denunciation. Then, as now, Robert had ridden at his back, offering quiet sympathy until he judged that Alec had wallowed long enough in his misery, then encouraging him to embrace his new destiny and move forward.

His horse splashed through a shallow stream that cut across the path, little more than an inch or two of water and so narrow that it could easily have been forded on foot had they been walking. On the far side the road forked, one path broadening out to become the main Shrewsbury road, the other doubling back into the forest and leading eventually to the small church of St. Edith, and the graveyard where Alexander McEwen had been interred alongside his parents. It was at this point that he and Robert had parted company three years ago, Robert carrying on toward Shrewsbury, while he had turned his horse's head to the gloomy woodland path to say his final farewell to the man who had once been as close as a father. Instead, he had been set upon by a pack of brigands who had identified themselves as Sun League, and who had spent countless days tormenting him until Robert had somehow found and rescued him.

Alec turned his head to see whether Robert remembered the place, but his words froze on his lips when he saw the dark shape of three approaching riders, the distinctive dark blue cloaks of the City Guard billowing around them. Cursing quietly, he signaled Robert with a toss of his head, then turned back in his saddle ready to spur his mount into action. He had no sooner tightened his grip on his reins, when three more riders emerged from the shadows of the forest, bearing down on them quickly.

Robert's shouted warning came a fraction of a second too late; before any of them could react, they found themselves surrounded on all sides by members of the City Guard. Alec recognized some of the men and had once counted their leader amongst his closest friends. It was he who spoke first.

"I hope you don't plan to make this difficult for us, Captain Weston."

Alec inclined his head. "Under the circumstances, I can't say I'm pleased to see you, Edmund."

"I, too, wish the circumstances had been different," Edmund said quietly. "I have orders to arrest you and your companions. Will you surrender your arms?"

Alec glanced to either side, where Robert and Kit flanked him, both looking grim and determined. "I fear I can't do that, Edmund," he said, unsheathing his sword. "I think we must see this through to the end."

He and Robert had fought side by side for many years and could confidently predict each other's moves, but Alec was surprised when Kit naturally fell into step, wheeling his mount sharply to the left just as Robert peeled off to the right. He in turn spurred his horse forward, so that within moments each of them was face to face with two of the City Guards.

After a few feints to either side, Alec kicked free of his stirrups and jumped to the ground just as his opponents did the same, hitting the dirt road a second ahead of them and giving him the time he needed to slice a low arc with his sword that swept the legs from beneath the younger of the Guards. He went down with a startled cry, clutching at the shallow cuts on both thighs, which, though not life-threatening, had effectively removed him from the fight.

Alec straightened to find Edmund almost upon him, sword raised, and he lifted his own blade and rebalanced himself, waiting for Edmund to make the first thrust. His opponent circled him warily. "It doesn't have to be like this, Alec," he said. "Throw down your weapons, and I swear you will be treated as befits your position."

Alec shrugged, dimly aware of his friends in roughly the same position, before a flurry of activity on both sides made the forest ring with clashing steel. He desperately wanted to turn his head and see the outcome, but he knew that Edmund was too skilled a swordsman for him to risk even a moment of inattention. "I trust you, my friend," he said. "It is your master I have no faith in."

Edmund nodded slightly, then sighed. "As you wish it," he said. He lunged forward, and it was only Alec's years of exhaustive training that allowed him to anticipate the move and parry it with agility. He leaned forward, shifting his weight to his right foot, then sliced his sword diagonally, though all he accomplished was to deal a bone-jarring blow to Edmund's well-placed weapon. The two of them traded furious blows for several moments, neither giving the other an inch of ground, and then both pulled back, panting harshly as they regrouped. Alec's previously wounded shoulder started throbbing with the sudden activity, but he resolutely ignored the pain.

The young Guard on the ground was still now, lying flat on his back, his face pale and greasy as a tallow candle. As Alec circled again, he saw that each of his friends had dealt similarly with one of their adversaries, so that all three of them were now facing a single foe. A hurried glance told Alec that Kit's opponent was a seasoned veteran who had been trained, as he had himself, by a master swordsman. He knew he could not allow himself to be distracted, but he couldn't help a sharp intake of breath when, out of the corner of his eye, he saw Kit throw himself into the attack.

He had to move fast to avoid a cutting thrust from Edmund's sword, but it was in that instant that he knew his opponent had overstepped. Edmund had put a little too much weight behind his thrust, and it overbalanced him very slightly. Another swordsman would likely not have profited from the error, but Alec had learned from the best, and was desperate enough besides. Although they traded several more rapid blows, Edmund was never able to regain his footing well enough, and Alec moved swiftly under his adversary's blade and dealt a glancing blow to Edmund's right side. Edmund yelled out a curse, although he kept tight hold of his sword, but Alec's next stab drove Edmund down onto his knees, and a second blow sliced through the lacings of his tunic and drew a thin line of blood from the base of Edmund's throat to an inch above his heart.

Even so, Edmund's sword continued to flail, until Alec's final thrust bit deeply into his wrist. He had no option but to drop his weapon, and the next moment, he froze as the tip of Alec's sword grazed the skin of his neck. His gaze flickered upward and met Alec's, and though he didn't give voice to a plea for mercy, the look on his face betrayed his longing for life.

"Call your men off," Alec demanded.

Edmund's eyes darted left and right, then he shrugged and lifted his hands, palms turned upward as though in supplication. Alec turned his head slightly and found that Robert was already trussing his two defeated opponents together with a length of frayed rope. He winked at Alec and gestured with his head, and Alec turned in time to see Kit attacking his adversary with a fierce onslaught of sword strokes that had the man stumbling blindly backward through the clearing. As his opponent faltered, Kit lunged and struck at the man's forearm with a savage downward stroke that Alec knew had not been taught by any fencing master. Kit's opponent dropped his sword with a loud curse, and a moment later, Kit's sword was wavering at the throat of the only City Guardsman left standing.

Alec turned his head back toward Edmund. "Well, my old friend," he said soberly, "it appears as though it is you who must surrender to me."

AS LUCK would have it, Robert had drawn the two least experienced Guards and had disarmed them quickly with no real effort and with little damage apart from a dent to their self-esteem. Kit had easily dealt with the first Guard he faced, although the second had required all of his skill, which, as Alec learned, was considerable.

It wasn't until the skirmish was over that Alec realized he had sustained a cut to the back of his hand and that Kit's left arm was slashed—a shallow but bloody wound that Robert hastily bandaged for him as soon as their opponents had been dealt with.

The defeated Guardsmen were now sitting on the patchy grass by the roadside, their wounds tended, their hands tied in front, and their weapons stacked in a neat pile just out of reach. Alec was gently rubbing a wet cloth across the slice on Edmund's chest, wiping away a thin trickle of blood.

"Can you tell me how you knew where to find us?" he asked.

Edmund grimaced as the cloth caught the ragged edge of his wound. He looked across the clearing at his men, not much the worse for their failed ambush attempt. "I suppose I owe you that much," he grunted. "There was an informant. Somebody who knew you would be traveling this path today. I don't know exactly what was discussed, but your name was spoken. His too," he said, gesturing toward Robert, who was standing a little way off.

Alec felt his mouth tighten in irritation. It seemed clear that Robert had said too much to the doxy he had tumbled the night before. No doubt she had hastened down to the barracks the minute Robert had left her bed, and before the sheets had even had time to cool she was selling him out for a groat or two. He turned away before Robert could read his displeasure, though he fully intended to tear a strip off the man when they were once more alone.

"Can you ride?" he asked Edmund.

"Aye," Edmund replied. He looked startled, as though he had not expected to be allowed to leave.

"Then I suggest you take your men and return to Ludlow," Alec said. He helped Edmund onto his feet, while Robert and Kit hoisted the others up with a tug under their armpits.

"We'll keep the weapons," Robert said. "Doubtless you'll be issued more when you return to the barracks." His voice was without expression, but the twinkle in his eyes showed he was well aware that there would be hell to pay for those soldiers unfortunate enough to return without their arms. For that reason, Alec returned Edmund's sword to him; he had fought valiantly and played them fair, and Alec still considered him a friend, despite landing on opposite sides of the issue at hand.

Before Edmund mounted his horse, Alec took him aside. "Tell Arlen's agents that we are leaving the shire," he said. "We are not a problem they need concern themselves with any longer."

Edmund shook his head. "I doubt it will do any good, not with a price on your heads, but I'll be glad to pass the message on." He laid his bandaged hand on Alec's arm. "Are you sure this is worth it?" he murmured. "We were instructed to bring the boy in alive. It seems as though Arlen considers him to be of some value. I'll warrant you could bargain for your lives with the lad's freedom, maybe even return to the Guard."

Alec glanced over at Kit, who was warily watching as Robert boosted each of the captive Guardsmen onto a horse and secured their bound hands to the pommel of their saddle. "My life in exchange for his liberty," he mused. He turned back and leveled a look at his friend. "It is not a bargain I care to make," he said steadily. "You may tell that to Arlen, if you get the chance."

Edmund snorted. "I'll have to do a whole lot better than that, my friend, if I am to save myself from patrolling the sheep fields for the rest of my days."

"I'm sorry it had to be you," Alec said, meaning it wholeheartedly. There were plenty in the City Guard he would have been only too pleased to send back to Ludlow in disgrace. But Edmund had always been a friend, and Alec disliked being the cause of his dishonor.

"No ill feelings," Edmund said. "I'll not forget that you held your sword to my throat but declined to take my life. I'm in your debt, Alec. We all are, though I doubt the youngsters will be pleased to be sent back with their tails between their legs."

"It will be a good lesson for them," Alec said dryly. He walked the short distance to Edmund's horse and helped him mount, then handed up the reins when his friend was seated. "Take care of yourself," he said.

"And you, Captain Weston," Edmund replied. "I hope the next time we meet the circumstances will be more favorable." He saluted smartly, then waved his men into single file and trotted away without looking back.

THEY had pushed hard, first changing direction in case they were followed, then galloping as fast as safety would allow, and riding on even after the sun had sunk behind the hills in the west and the path was too dark to see beyond the end of their horses' muzzles.

Finally Alec called a halt and led them off the single track and deep into the forest, where they were now huddled around a small fire, eating the food Francis had packed for them. Though Alec knew it was the finest quality and doubtless delicious, he tasted little of it.

He waited until Kit lay down and rolled himself into the cloak he'd borrowed from Jamie's well-stocked clothes press before he turned his gaze on Robert's preoccupied face. He'd had time to calm down and was no longer as angry as he'd been this morning. Robert rarely made mistakes; he could be forgiven this one slip.

"I imagine next time you'll want to keep the exchange of sweet nothings brief," he said, because Robert would not expect him to let the error pass without at least some acknowledgment.

Robert raised his eyes from the flickering fire and looked at him blankly.

"Your late-night visit," Alec clarified. "It appears your lady friend was a little too anxious to share your whereabouts with the Guard."

Robert's eyes widened. "You think it was Kathleen sold us out?" he asked.

Alec shrugged. "It wouldn't be the first time a bawd had profited from a secret shared between the sheets."

Robert nodded. "As you say," he agreed. "Except that the only thing I shared with Kathleen was a fleeting moment of release. Everything else, I kept to myself."

Alec frowned. "You didn't even tell her your name? There was enough talk about us in Ludlow that she'd have recognized the chance to earn a little extra."

"Alec, what do you take me for?" Robert said, though he sounded weary rather than outraged. "I barely spoke two words to the girl. I certainly didn't share our travel plans!"

The firewood crackled as the burnt branches collapsed, sending sparks shooting into the air. In the distance, an owl hooted, the only other sound, apart from Kit's steady, rhythmic breathing.

"Nobody knew we traveled today," Alec said, frowning at Robert.

Robert met his gaze squarely. "Jamie knew. And he knew that we were heading in this direction."

"Jamie is beyond reproach," Alec said tightly.

Robert arched an eyebrow. "I don't wish to think ill of him…."

"Beyond reproach," Alec repeated distinctly. He held Robert's gaze, letting all of his conviction show, until Robert dropped his eyes with a shrug.

Alec felt a growing sense of disquiet as he turned over the recent events in his mind. He wondered if it was possible that Jamie had innocently shared their plans, perhaps with his notary, Thomas Marchant, or with some other business acquaintance whose help he had sought. Although Jamie didn't know the exact route they were taking, he knew their final destination and knew which ship they would board and when.

"Do you think it safe to continue on to Boston?" Robert asked, his mind obviously traveling the same path as Alec's.

Alec pulled in a deep breath. "I doubt we've seen the last of the Guard, and next time we might not be so lucky. And I'm convinced the Sun League is still on the prowl." He looked into Robert's dark eyes. "I don't see that we have much option but to continue."

Robert inclined his head stiffly. "Then we must put our lives in Jamie McEwen's hands," he said.

CHAPTER 8

IT WAS the first time since leaving Ludlow that they had ventured into anything larger than a village. For two days they had kept to the narrow trails and wooded back roads, glad to leave Salop behind them and cross the unmarked border into the rolling countryside of Staffordshire. Even then they had kept off the main route as much as possible, weaving their way through tiny hamlets until they reached the market town of Lichfield.

In the early hours of the morning, they crossed over the defensive ditch that ringed the town, and rode through the wooden gate at Sandford Street with no more than a cursory glance from the gatekeeper, whose main job was to ensure that merchants entering the town paid the correct toll on their goods and who had little interest in three riders with barely a saddlebag between them.

After nights spent huddled in forest clearings or crowded together in squalid wayside hostelries, Alec had insisted that they spend some of their funds on decent accommodations in one of the better inns, and they were now settled in a small but serviceable room in the Royal Oak on Quoniames Lane.

Robert had dumped his satchel on the pallet beside the large bed and gone straight back out to scout the area, promising to return when darkness fell and join them for supper. For the first time since they had begun their travels together, Alec felt it was safe for him and Kit to venture out, so moments after Robert left, they, too, descended the wooden staircase and walked out into the sunshine.

Kit strolled beside Alec as they turned left onto Dam Street, looking about with interest. To the north, the three spires of the cathedral rose above the town, its red sandstone casting a warm glow in the sunlight. Pilgrims were already thronging the street, making their way to the chapel that housed the relics of St. Chad, the Bishop of Mercia who had founded the original cathedral over six hundred years ago.

"Do you want to take a look?" Alec asked.

Kit shook his head. He hadn't set foot inside a church for years, ever since Marcus had taken him from his home. Up until that point, his family had been pious enough, attending Mass every Sunday as expected, but de Crecy had declared he had no time for such things, although, surprisingly, some of his followers seemed devout. After a year of living with Marcus, Kit had been asked if he wanted to attend services with some of the men whose families were still faithful, but he had declined, feeling at that point he was beyond redemption.

"Unless you want to visit?" Kit offered.

Alec eyed him closely, and then he, too, shook his head. "I'd rather take a walk this fine morning," he said. "Come, let's see what Lichfield has to offer."

They made their way to Robe Street, bordering the market square, and spent an hour wandering about the numerous stalls that offered all manner of foodstuffs, worked leather, and bolts of fine, richly dyed cloth. Alec purchased a round loaf of bread and two apples, which they ate happily as they meandered along, watching housewives bargain loudly with the traders, young boys playing amongst the wooden stalls, and several Grey Friars from the substantial Franciscan estate nearby hurrying about their business.

As they rounded the corner onto Newebrugge Street, Kit froze at the sight of two members of the City Guard standing in the shade of a door lintel and idly watching the passersby. He shivered as sunlight glinted off their sharpened steel swords, and picked out the swan device that was embroidered onto their woolen cloaks, but a moment later, he felt strong fingers firmly grasp his elbow, and Alec smiled tightly and guided him past the guards' position without so much as a glance in their direction.

"We're not known here," he murmured, once they had successfully navigated the way. "It's doubtful we'll be recognized."

Kit breathed a sigh of relief, feeling tension ease from his stiff shoulders. Alec kept his hand cupped around Kit's elbow as they walked, and Kit felt a sense of security wash through him like a wave.

Alec steered them through the doorway of a tavern and into a tiny courtyard out back, no more than three small tables perched on top of some weathered wooden planking, but shaded and pleasant, more so when the innkeeper followed them out and deposited a pitcher of cold wine in front of them.

Kit swallowed a deep draft of the sweet white wine, then wiped his mouth with the back of his hand. Alec was watching him with an amused look in his eyes.

"Not quite as good as Jamie's cellar," he said, "but decent enough." Alec tipped his own mug and drank with obvious relish.

"How far to Boston, do you think?" Kit asked.

Alec shrugged. "Not above three more days, if our luck holds," he replied. "Robert is making some inquiries about the safest route."

"Have you and Robert known each other long?" Kit asked.

A faint smile slid across Alec's face. "He took me in hand when I first joined the Guard," he said. "I was as green as yonder leaves, although I thought I knew everything, of course," he continued, chuckling quietly. "He set me straight on a number of issues, and he taught me pretty much everything worth knowing."

"And he truly doesn't mind leaving England on my account?" Kit pressed. He had lived amongst the cruelest, most pitiless men in the kingdom for so long that it was difficult to accept that there were people who did not put their own interests first and who were motivated by righteousness instead of greed.

Alec's smile grew wider. "Robert's integrity is without equal," he said. "If I have any small amount of principle, it is largely due to him."

Kit doubted that was true. From what he'd heard about Alec's past, it appeared as though he'd always acted selflessly and with honor, even in the face of falsehood and animosity.

"And what of you?" Alec asked softly. "Do you mind leaving behind all you've known to travel to a foreign land?"

Kit pondered the question for a moment. If he'd been asked before his father's death, he suspected his answer might be different, but three years in the company of the Sun League had stripped away so much of what had been decent and good in his life, and his recent meeting with his mother had shown him that there was no going back. He didn't harbor the slightest doubt.

"I want to start afresh," he said fervently, looking into Alec's deep-set eyes. "I want to leave that old life far behind and never look back." He stopped suddenly, unsure whether to voice the rest, but decided in the end that it needed saying. "I'm happy that you and Robert chose to accompany me. None of this would have much meaning without you," he said shyly.

Alec picked up his mug and drained the contents, all the while keeping his eyes fixed on Kit's face. When he finished, he lowered the mug and placed it carefully back on the table. "I hope you realize that you don't owe us anything," he said, his brows drawing together in a frown. "If I thought you felt indebted in any way—"

"But I do," Kit interrupted.

"We both made our choices freely," Alec said firmly. His tone softened as he continued. "Robert has spent half his life in the Guard, so you know that his decision was not taken lightly. As always, he followed the path of true justice."

"And you?" Kit asked, hoping to hear a different reason.

"My decision was rather less noble," Alec admitted, his eyes alive with feeling. "Though you owe me nothing, all the same."

Though he vehemently disagreed with his friend, Kit allowed the silence between them to lengthen, until Alec eventually changed the subject. Perhaps Alec didn't fully understand what Kit's life had been like before he and Robert came along—because if he did, he'd know that Kit owed him everything.

He watched Alec's soft lips move as he spoke, only half listening to the words but captivated by the animation on the man's face. Alec's ready smile flashed constantly, and his eyes brimmed with humor and warmth. When Marcus de Crecy had turned his steely gaze onto Kit's face, Kit had always shuddered in dread, knowing that the man would soon be making sickening demands of him. Kit realized with a sudden stark clarity that despite Alec's feelings for him, his friend would never press his suit or make any claims, and it touched something deep inside, something Kit thought had been damaged beyond the ability to heal. Almost without thought, he reached across the table and covered Alec's hand with his own, and those deep blue eyes widened in surprise.

"I'm very glad you're here," Kit said. *"With me,"* he emphasized. His heart fluttered wildly as Alec turned his hand over and grasped Kit's fingers. He could feel the calluses that had been made by Alec's sword, and he gripped the hand more tightly.

"I'll be here, whether you want more from this or not," Alec promised.

"I want more," Kit blurted, as sure as he'd ever felt about anything in his life. "Will you return to the tavern with me?" he asked tentatively, feeling a hot blush flame across his cheekbones.

Alec inclined his head, considering him closely, and Kit sat still under the scrutiny, hoping that his friend would be able to read his inarticulate longing. "Are you sure you know what you are asking?" Alec finally said.

Kit nodded wordlessly, his mouth drying as a painful thought struck him. "If you still want me?" he asked hesitantly.

Alec closed his eyes and pulled in a sharp breath. "With all my heart," he whispered. He leaned forward, his piercing eyes fixing intently on Kit's face. "But I must be sure that you offer freely," he said.

Kit clenched his fingers around Alec's. "With all my heart," he echoed. He held his breath, gratified beyond words when Alec nodded.

"Then I'll happily accept," he said simply.

THEY walked side by side along the narrow lanes and crowded streets, not speaking much, but content in each other's company. From time to time, Kit glanced at Alec's serene profile, his blood stirring each time they inadvertently brushed against each other.

Halfway back to the Royal Oak, the skies opened and a downpour drenched them to the skin. Laughing, they ran back to the tavern as fast as they could, and tumbled through the doorway just as lightning began to flash overhead. Kit followed Alec up the staircase and into their shared room, pulling his damp shirt off and turning just as Alec did the same. Alec rubbed his shirt absently through his wet hair, faltering slightly when their eyes met.

Kit's gaze traveled the length of Alec's torso, watching the play of taut muscles under smooth, sun-darkened skin. He closed the distance between them and gently disentangled Alec's fingers before dropping Alec's sodden shirt onto the floor at their feet.

He reached a tentative hand and traced one of the scars on Alec's chest, the cool skin warming under his touch. Alec pulled in a sharp breath and tensed.

Kit tipped his head and met Alec's eyes again, their color dark with emotion, and he leaned in and brushed his lips against Alec's, tasting the sticky residue of sweet wine. Alec moved his hands to rest lightly on Kit's hips, neither grasping nor tugging him forward, simply anchoring him to the spot while Alec deepened the kiss. Kit stepped forward anyway, his groin brushing against the swell of

Alec's breeches, and he raised his arms to circle Alec's back and press their cool, damp skin together.

Alec broke the kiss and drew his head back a little, looking deeply into Kit's eyes. "Are you absolutely sure you want this?" he asked, his voice husky.

In reply Kit dragged Alec's hand off his hip and pushed it down until it cupped his prick, hot and hard and straining against the fabric of his breeches. He groaned when Alec ran strong fingers up its pulsing length and bent his head to press their lips together once again.

They stumbled toward the bed, still locked in each other's arms, and Alec lowered him carefully onto the stained coverlet, then rolled up beside him. He brushed his hand over Kit's scarred body, and Kit stiffened unconsciously and turned his head away.

Alec froze. "I would never do anything you did not wish," he whispered, close against Kit's ear.

Kit risked a glance at Alec's face, realizing that Alec had read reluctance where Kit felt only shame.

"These marks are his," he stammered, because he had never been able to look at them or feel them throb without thinking of the man who had carved them there.

Alec laced his fingers through Kit's and tugged gently until Kit's hand was splayed across Alec's chest. Kit felt the ridges left by the Sun League's whips press against his palm, and the tension as Alec's body stiffened. Looking more closely, he saw that his friend's mouth had tightened and that a vein in his temple throbbed rhythmically, and Kit suddenly saw what his own experience should have made clear: underneath the bravado, Alec felt as deeply troubled by his own markings as Kit.

The thought that this man of honor could feel in any way disgraced or sullied broke through the humiliation and feeling of worthlessness that had festered in Kit since he'd first been claimed by Marcus de Crecy.

He had fretted about what he could give Alec that was worthy of the man, only now realizing that Alec needed the same thing he did: somebody who understood and accepted, somebody with whom to share the most profound trust and most intimate of dreams.

Wordlessly pulling his friend down, he offered himself unconditionally for the first time in his life, giving freely to Alec what had only ever been torn from him by force.

"WHERE'S the boy?"

Alec looked up from his seat beside the fireplace as Robert walked into the great hall, bringing a blast of fresh air with him.

"He's upstairs sleeping," he replied.

Robert pulled up a chair and gestured to the innkeeper, who nodded and disappeared into the small back storage room. Robert turned his perceptive gaze on Alec, who tried his best not to squirm. Nonetheless, he had the uncomfortable feeling that Robert knew exactly how he'd spent the past hour.

"You don't look any worse for the storm," Alec said, hoping to distract his friend.

"I found shelter quickly enough," Robert replied, murmuring his thanks as the innkeeper placed a flagon of foaming beer in front of him. "Is that wise?" he asked bluntly, his chin lifting to indicate the staircase, and beyond that, their shared room where Kit had fallen asleep after lovemaking.

Alec wasn't about to pretend he didn't know what Robert was talking about.

He shrugged. "Is the heart ever wise?" he asked.

"Not always," Robert agreed. "Which is why the head must be allowed to rule."

Alec accepted the rebuke wordlessly.

"The Sun League is about," Robert said, and Alec felt the languorous afterglow of passion dissipate in an instant. Though Robert had refrained from pressing home the point, he was right: Alec had been foolish to start anything with Kit before they were safely out of the reach of both the City Guard and the Sun League.

"Do they know we're here?" he asked tightly.

Robert arched an eyebrow. "I'd hardly be sitting here discussing the weather if they did," he said sardonically. "There are two of them. They seem to be taking no pains to disguise themselves."

"They rarely do, unless they feel threatened."

Alec turned his head at the sound of Kit's voice. The young man was standing at the bottom of the staircase, looking slightly disheveled though otherwise alert. He crossed the few steps toward the fireplace, hooking the rung of a low stool with his boot as he moved, and joined the two of them at the table. He flashed a shy smile at Alec before turning his attention back to Robert. "You must have realized this in your dealings with the League. People are terrified of them. Everybody in the shire knew who Marcus was, yet we traveled about unchallenged."

"I understand the force of their influence in the smaller villages," Robert said. "I just thought they'd hold less sway in a town like this."

"Most people have something they wish to protect," Kit said. "Town or village, the same principle applies." He bit down on his lip and ducked his head.

"I suspect you saw a lot of things with de Crecy that you'd rather not have," Robert said quietly.

"He was not always… subtle," Kit replied. He raised his head and met Robert's gaze. "But I doubt I've seen worse than you," he said evenly.

Alec started in surprise, wondering when Robert had shared any of his past with Kit. He had heard some of it, usually late at night over several tankards of ale, and it had not always been a pretty tale. Robert's former master, Roger Mortimer, had been a brilliant, accomplished, highly skilled courtier who had risen to dizzying heights; he had also been a tyrannical, overbearing traitor who had deposed one king and tried to dominate another.

When pushed, Alec had balked at Anthony Arlen's high-handed command, but Robert and Kit had spent years under the influence of powerful, degenerate men, and Alec wondered briefly whether their common experience allowed them to understand each other in ways that he never could.

"I don't think they're here looking for you," Robert said, dispelling the gloom that had settled over the table. "I doubt the danger is immediate. It's probably best if we get a good night of sleep and slip away first thing in the morning."

Alec agreed, and after waving the innkeeper over, he ordered a rich supper and asked for a bottle of wine. While Robert and Kit drank their fill, he barely wet his lips; though he trusted Robert's assessment of the situation, he thought it wise that one of them keep a clear head. Besides, troubling recollections had been stirred for both his friends, and he thought it only fair that they should be afforded the luxury of dulled wits and blunted memory and the chance for a night of easy rest.

He leaned over and refilled both their glasses, ignoring their protests. With the road ahead still so unknown, there was no guessing when any of them would enjoy another peaceful night.

KIT woke from a deep sleep to find the room shrouded in the pitch-black of night. He could feel Alec's solid presence at his back, his arms cradling Kit in a loose embrace. Deep inside he felt an ache, insistent though not unpleasant, and his heart thundered as he remembered Alec's thick cock moving inside him, erasing the memory of Marcus de Crecy and replacing it with something infinitely more joyful.

He sighed in pure pleasure and started to roll over, but stopped with a muffled cry when pain shot through him as the stripes Marcus had laid across his back rubbed against the rough cotton sheet, the insistent throb a counterpoint to the ache he had been contemplating so blissfully.

A chill spread through his limbs, reaching into every part of him, reminding him all over again that though he might run, though he might leave England behind and travel to the ends of the earth, he would never truly be free of Marcus de Crecy, not when his own body bore witness to Marcus's eternal hold over him.

CHAPTER 9

WITH the sighting of the Sun League fresh in his mind, Alec made the decision to push harder on the final leg of their journey. He reckoned it would be easier to hide in the bustling port of Boston while they waited for their ship rather than to travel through the sparsely populated hamlets that lined the route, where strangers were more conspicuous.

For that reason, he had persuaded Robert and Kit to abandon the safe but slower back roads and instead set their mounts on the main road from Lichfield to Boston. They struck out on the northeast road that would take them first to Burton before they would swing south again to link with the main road east into Lincolnshire. They joined a steady stream of merchants, laborers, itinerant preachers, messengers, and pilgrims, traveling on foot or on horseback, driving pack animals laden with merchandise or steering great two-wheeled carts that groaned under the weight of sacks of wool or crates of dried goods.

They reached Burton just as the sun was setting, and secured an overnight stay with the Benedictine monks of St. Modwen's Abbey. They had to share the great hall with a dozen other travelers, but Alec thought that would probably suit his companions better than a more private accommodation. Robert would be glad to see that Alec was once more letting his head rule his heart, and Alec couldn't help but notice that Kit had been ominously quiet all day.

He cursed himself for being a fool, for pushing Kit before he was really ready to consider a deeper commitment. He had woken this morning to find Kit already up and dressed and out of the room, and the young man had kept to himself since setting off from Lichfield, sitting his mount stiffly and shying away from company.

Alec watched surreptitiously as Kit threw his bedroll onto one of the pallets that had been spread out on the flagstone floor of the monastery's hall, claiming a space as close to the door as he could get.

"What's wrong with him?"

Robert's voice sounded close to his ear, and Alec turned his head to find his old friend watching Kit, a frown creasing his forehead.

"I'm not sure," Alec replied.

"If it's something between the two of you, you'd better fix it," Robert said flatly.

Supper consisted of a small bowl of boiled mutton and cabbage washed down with watered ale, the abbey being a poor outpost with few facilities. Whether it was due to the meager fare or the fatigue of the travelers, there was little conversation at the long trestle table that had been set up in a narrow hallway leading from the kitchen, and afterward, there being nothing else to do, most of the men returned to the hall and settled down for an early night.

Alec followed Robert, who dragged his pallet closer to Kit's and rolled himself into a coarse woolen blanket, scarcely saying good night before dropping off to sleep. Kit turned his back and huddled under his own blankets, and Alec took the hint and refrained from speaking, though he burned to know what was troubling his young companion.

He tossed and turned, unable to get comfortable, listening to the sounds of men settling in for the night. Finally he gave up and rolled off the pallet. He picked his way carefully around the sleeping forms stretched out in all directions and made his way through the heavy oak doors at the back of the monastery and into a cloister whose open sides bordered a verdant courtyard.

The bright moon lit the way, its light augmented by torches burning at regular intervals in wall sconces. Alec strolled the length of the cloister, breathing in the scent of rosemary and mint, an aroma that reminded him of Jamie's garden in Ludlow. He stopped when he came to a low stone bench, and settling down on its cool surface, he leaned back against the wall and closed his eyes, enjoying the fragrant air and the memories it stirred in him.

Outside of Alexander's study, the garden had been his and Jamie's favorite place to roam. They had spent many hours sneaking into the orchard and gorging on apples and crunchy pears, seeing who could balance longest atop the high stone walls, and practicing the quarterstaff with branches cut from the fruit trees. It had been a magical time, their happiness at being together so pure and all consuming.

"You look content."

Alec's eyes flew open at Kit's soft voice, and he looked up to find his friend standing beside the bench, a small smile on his lips.

"Some happy memories," Alec replied, shrugging.

"Would you mind if I join you?" Kit asked, sounding almost shy. "Unless you'd rather not be disturbed," he added quickly.

"Of course not. Sit," Alec said.

Kit sat down beside him, his eyes trained on the courtyard ahead. A stray lock of hair was stuck to his cheek, and Alec's fingers tingled, itching to reach out and smooth it back. But he knew the intimate gesture was ill-advised, particularly in a place like this, and he was not sure that Kit would welcome his touch.

"You were very quiet today," he said instead.

"Was I?" Kit replied, sounding faintly surprised.

Alec swallowed hard, then gathered his courage and plunged ahead. "I fear you have had cause to regret our intimacy."

Kit didn't reply immediately, and Alec's stomach did a slow, nauseating roll. "I shouldn't have pushed so fast," he murmured. "You were not ready."

Kit turned his head, his expression lost in the shadowy darkness. "Is that what you think?" he asked, the surprised tone stronger now. "I've never been so sure of anything in my life."

Alec couldn't deny the feeling of relief that coursed through him. "So what was troubling you all day?" he asked.

"I...." Kit trailed off, biting his lip so hard that Alec was afraid he might draw blood.

"What is it, Kit?" Alec asked, panic beginning to rise.

"I'm not who you think I am," Kit blurted. "I've done terrible things—"

"Things you were forced to," Alec interrupted.

"Is that any defense?" Kit whispered. "I spent three years with the Sun League. I rode along on their raids. I thieved for them. You know what I was to Marcus." His hand moved to cover his heart, unconsciously rubbing the tattoo that branded him. "Sometimes I think I'll always be theirs," he said bleakly.

Alec felt pity flood him, the desolation in Kit's voice touching him deeply. "You would never have done those things if you'd had the choice," he said gently. "Do you not think there is forgiveness for something that was beyond your control?"

Silence fell again as Kit seemed to consider how to answer the question. He scrubbed at his cheek, absently tucking the stray lock of hair behind his ear, and Alec felt his blood stir when he remembered the short, soft strands slipping through his fingers like silk. Alec forced his eyes away, letting them drift over the glazed earthenware tiles under his feet and the intricate pattern etched into them. A sudden thought struck him, and he forgot his previous caution and placed his hand on Kit's arm. "Are you afraid?" he asked.

A flash of white revealed Kit's teeth, though whether in a smile or a grimace was hard to ascertain. "I'd be a damned fool if I wasn't," he replied. He leaned back, and the shadows swallowed him further.

Alec was about to press him for clarification when the cloister door opened and one of the monks stepped out. He hastily withdrew his hand from Kit's arm and nodded a greeting as the old monk walked toward them.

"Good evening," the monk said, inclining his head. He stopped and glanced out across the courtyard and into the night sky. "I think there's a storm coming in," he said, and indeed, dark clouds were gathering overhead. "Do you have far to go?"

"We travel east, brother," Kit replied, subtly sidestepping the question.

"You travel for business?" the monk asked.

"Aye," Kit said shortly, allowing the pause to lengthen until it was obvious that he meant to say nothing more.

"You are merchants, perhaps?" the old man inquired. "There are many traders traveling this route."

"We take what work we can find," Kit said vaguely. "I hope you have a pleasant evening, brother," he continued, dismissing the old man politely but firmly.

The monk shrugged, accepting Kit's rebuff with good grace. "God be with you both," he said. He turned and made his way slowly back the way he'd come, before disappearing behind the door with a quick backward glance.

"You're very skilled at evasion," Alec observed.

Kit leaned his head back against the wall, tipping his face upward so the light from a nearby torch illuminated his features. "The League would not scruple to torment a holy brother if they thought he had any information," he said softly. "It was for his own benefit."

Alec felt a chill pass through him that had nothing to do with the impending storm. "Do you fear that de Crecy will chase you down himself?" he asked.

"I doubt he would," Kit said, perhaps a little too quickly.

Alec cast a sidelong glance at Kit's face, but it was hard to read anything in the dull light.

"I'm tired," Kit said suddenly. "I think I'll turn in for the night."

Though it was clear to Alec that Kit was trying to avoid any further questions, he nevertheless rose and followed his friend down the walkway, and when they reached the door leading back into the monastery, he called Kit's name. The young man reluctantly turned.

Casting about quickly to ensure they were not overlooked, Alec reached a hand to Kit's face. He was not foolish enough to make promises he could not keep, but as he stroked his thumb across Kit's high cheekbone, he murmured, "Try not to worry about de Crecy. Robert and I will be with you, whatever may come."

A small, sad smile lifted the corner of Kit's mouth as he briefly leaned into Alec's hand. "Don't you see?" he whispered. "That's precisely what I'm worried about."

As THE old monk had predicted, the next day the heavens opened and rain began to fall. By the time the horses were saddled and packed, Kit was already miserably cold and wet, and hours later, after a steady downpour that refused to let up, he was soaked right through to the skin.

His mount plodded along the cinder track, splashing through puddles and the increasingly cloying mud, following Alec and Robert in slow single file. Kit's damp undershirt stuck to his chilled skin, water dripped incessantly from the brim of his cap, and his sodden cloak was getting wetter and heavier with every passing league. It was precious little consolation that the road was practically empty, and for the first time in days they didn't have to worry about running into the Sun League or the City Guard, since neither party would be foolish enough to be abroad in this weather.

Alec didn't want to stop to eat, so they had to settle for a hunk of the coarse black bread that the monks had packed for them, chewing morosely while they kept to their saddles and the slate-gray sky gradually darkened overhead. Finally, even Alec accepted that unless the weather improved, they couldn't continue much longer. He promised to pull off the road at the first opportunity, so Kit tugged his soggy cap down as far as it would go, turned up the collar of his cloak, and hunched down low, trying to make the best of his sorry lot.

He regretted having lied to Alec about Marcus, although he didn't think his friend had actually believed him. Kit was in no doubt that Marcus himself would be leading the search for him and that he would comb the country from shore to shore in order to find him. Marcus's pride was a living, breathing thing, and any wound to it would have to be paid for in full. Kit carried the scars from the last time he had run out on Marcus, together with the threat that still rung in his ears.

He'd been driven to his hands and knees, blood pooling on the dirty rushes underneath him, his back cut to ribbons and burning as though it had been set ablaze. Marcus had casually looped the long leather lash around the handle of his whip and crouched down beside him, tapping his chin gently to make him raise his tear-stained face.

"Don't make me come looking for you again," he had said mildly, though the words had still sent dread coursing through Kit's body. Marcus had leaned in then, brushing away the salty tears that dripped down Kit's face like today's rain, and had kissed him softly on his bloodied lips. "I wouldn't like to lose you," he had added, the warning as clear as if he'd directly threatened Kit's life. Later that night he had been uncharacteristically solicitous and gentle, though his attentions had still opened up the scabs on Kit's back, and would continue to do so for more than a week to come.

Kit shifted uncomfortably in the saddle. Something he had not lied to Alec about was his fear. Marcus was not a man to give up easily, whatever the odds, and Kit couldn't help but wonder whether sooner or later he would have to face the consequences of running once again. What disturbed his sleep, though, was the fate in store for the two men who had helped him. He had too often witnessed the results of Marcus's vengeance, and it chilled his soul to think of that cruelty turned against his friends.

Up ahead, a thin plume of smoke spiraled into the damp air, and Kit's spirits rose a little when Alec signaled that they would leave the road and follow the narrow track to a farmhouse some few hundred yards off in the distance. They turned their mounts onto the muddy path and plodded slowly up to a courtyard, surrounded on three sides by low wooden buildings. As they halted, a door opened and a man appeared and waved a hand in greeting.

Alec leaned forward and raised his voice to overcome the beating rain. "Would you be able to spare some food and shelter?" he asked. "We are able to pay."

"You are welcome to share whatever we have," the man said. He pointed to the building to his right. "You can stable your animals there if you want. There's plenty of feed."

Kit swung off his horse, gratefully stretching his cramped muscles. He trudged to the barn, avoiding the chickens pecking in the dirt, and together he and Robert unsaddled the mounts and rubbed them down with handfuls of hay, while Alec discreetly saw to payment. When accounts were settled, they followed the man, whose name they learned was Giles Beck, crowding across his threshold and into the single room that served as kitchen, bedchamber, and storage room. The air in the room was thick with smoke, drifting up from the open fireplace and curling under the leaky thatch. It smelled of boiled cabbage and damp wool, and underneath that, the faint odor of unwashed bodies too long penned indoors.

In one corner of the room, on a pallet on the floor, three young children huddled together under a torn blanket, their great round eyes peering out of the gloom. Giles introduced his wife, Mary, a plain, plump woman who balanced a baby on her hip while she stirred the contents of a three-legged iron pot that stood over the fireplace. Her face was flushed with heat, and the room was so warm that Kit's wet clothes, already dripping great puddles onto the dirt floor, began to steam.

Mrs. Beck smiled shyly. "You should get some of those damp clothes off," she suggested. "If you hang them by the fire, they'll be a little drier when you leave."

Kit hurried to pull off his cloak, and they all folded their clothing over the back of a wooden chair, then dragged it in front of the fireplace.

"Please sit," Mrs. Beck said, indicating a long wooden bench that was set beside the kitchen table. She deftly set trenchers in front of each of them, then, still balancing her child, ladled pottage from the cooking pot into a bowl and placed it in the middle of the table before distributing chunks of dark bread to the three children sitting mutely in the corner. Kit realized that he was famished, though he was careful not to take too much from the bowl in case it was all the family had. As though reading his thoughts, Mrs. Beck urged him on, refilling his trencher when he would have laid his spoon aside.

Giles Beck, who was sitting opposite Alec on an upturned barrel, filled his stomach quickly before turning his attention to his guests. "Where do you hail from, sirs?" he asked.

"We've recently been in Ludlow," Alec replied.

"What news from town?" Beck asked. "We seldom leave the farm except to attend market. News is hard to come by."

Alec shrugged. "We were there only briefly," he said apologetically. "There is talk of trouble with France."

Giles waved a hand dismissively. "That is hardly news," he said, smiling faintly. "We always seem to be at odds with somebody or the other."

"I suppose that sort of thing doesn't trouble you much out here?" Robert asked.

"War with France, war with Scotland, it's all the same to us. The only thing we fear is the return of the *maltolte*. Two years ago the King demanded an extra ten shillings on each sack of wool that was exported. The buyers preserve their profit by paying us less for our product. We already pay a hefty tax on our wool, any more makes for a hard life."

Kit glanced around the humble shack, wondering how things could get much harder than this. His own family had lived modestly, but there had been meat for the table and room enough for all of them.

He realized that whatever misfortune he had endured with Marcus de Crecy, it had at least been a world of plenty, filled with the kind of luxuries that he had come to take for granted and that these hardworking people could only dream about.

Alec was shaking his head. "I fear I bring bad news, then," he said. "A merchant friend in Ludlow has been summoned to a meeting in Nottingham in September. He is of the mind that the tithe will be reintroduced to pay for the coming war."

Giles exchanged a look with his wife, and it was clear to see the fear that flashed briefly across their faces before resignation set in.

"We must accept that the King does all for the best," Giles sighed. "Will you stay the night?" he asked. "The rain isn't likely to let up for a good while, and you'll not find an inn for miles."

Kit didn't relish the thought of sharing the cramped space with the family, although he was touched by their readiness to extend hospitality to strangers. He was heartened when Giles continued, "There's fresh hay in the barn, if you don't mind bedding down with the animals."

Alec and Robert rose, and Kit hastily followed.

"We'll gladly take you up on the offer," Robert said. He turned to Mary and smiled warmly. "Thank you for supper, Mistress Beck," he said sincerely, and Kit saw once more a flash of the kind heart that Robert tried, and so often failed, to conceal.

The cold air was welcome after the fetid dampness, although Kit still hurried across the muddy courtyard and into the barn. It was cooler here, and the smell of wet hide and manure was heavy, but it was preferable to crowding together in the smoke-filled hovel. Giles showed them to an empty stall, its floor lined with fresh hay, and left them with the light of a single candle stub, wishing them good night as he closed the barn door behind him. After a moment to orient himself, Alec extinguished the candle; moonlight was filtering through the cracks in the walls and ceiling, enough to see all they needed.

They had left their dripping cloaks to dry in front of the dying embers of the fireplace, so they all three burrowed into the hay, tucking it around them as tightly as they could and huddling together to conserve heat. The wind whistled through the crumbling daub walls, but for now it was warm enough, lying this closely to each other, Kit sandwiched between Robert and Alec and feeling luckiest of all of them.

Robert was lying on his back, his head cradled on his folded arms. "I wonder if King Edward has the first notion of what his wars mean to ordinary folk," he mused.

Alec snorted. "Doubtful," he said, rolling up onto his side and looking at his friend over Kit's recumbent body. "As long as he gets his tax and the men he needs to fight, I doubt he concerns himself with the rest of his people."

"The nobility. They're all the same," Robert mumbled bitterly. "They care nothing for the common man." He turned onto his side, his back toward Kit, and moments later his breathing evened out and he was asleep.

"He's always been able to do that," Alec murmured, sounding impressed.

"The sleep of the innocent," Kit whispered. "That's what my mother called it, anyway."

Alec raised an eyebrow. "I've heard him called many things," he said softly. "But I doubt 'innocent' could be counted among them."

Kit turned his head, watching Alec's face under the glow of the moonlight. "He told me he was Mortimer's man," he said. "That must have been… eventful," he finished lamely, unable to find words that did not sound judgmental.

"Aye," Alec nodded. "He saw the best and the worst of that man. He followed Mortimer into exile and lived as a barely tolerated guest in a foreign land, then returned with an invading army and lived like a king. And in the end, Mortimer was nothing more than a traitor, his body left to rot like a carcass on a butcher's shamble."

Kit shuddered, horror vying with sympathy.

Alec glanced over Kit's shoulder at Robert's hunched back. "He was there at the end," he said sadly. "The only one of Mortimer's men who stayed with him. He followed the cart on foot, all the way from the Tower to Tyburn. He witnessed the whole thing—Mortimer was hung, drawn, and quartered, and the pieces left in the open for two days before his body was claimed." He shook his head. "And when Robert returned to Ludlow to report back to the Lady Joan, she dismissed him, along with all of her husband's retainers, as though they could somehow be held to account for what their master had done."

"I suppose it was painful for her to be reminded," Kit said, although it seemed a callous way of behaving to men and women who were blameless.

Alec laughed mirthlessly. "She received a taste of her own medicine," he said. "All of Mortimer's lands and possessions were forfeit to the crown. She lost Ludlow and most of her titles and holdings. Robert is right," he continued, shaking his head. "They are, all of them, cut from the same cloth."

IN THE middle of the night, Kit woke to find that the temperature had dropped and he was shivering violently, even though sheltered on both sides by his friends. He squirmed closer to Alec, breathing deeply of the smell of leather, dried sweat, and the dust from countless days in the saddle, but unable to leech any more warmth from Alec's body.

Behind him he heard a rustling sound, and looking over his shoulder, he saw that Robert had arisen and was walking down the line of stalls, peering into each in turn. When he returned, he was dragging a tattered blanket, stinking of horse flesh and riddled with holes, but heavy and warm for all that. Without a word he threw the blanket over Kit's quivering body and dropped back onto the hay, tucking himself tightly against Kit's back.

By the time Kit's teeth had stopped chattering long enough to murmur his thanks, Robert had fallen back into deep sleep.

CHAPTER 10

SITUATED three miles upstream on the banks of the River Witham, Boston was one of the busiest ports in all the kingdom, and as Alec hurried past imposing Mediterranean galleys and cogs from northern Europe, a flotilla of skiffs bobbing between them, it was easy to believe that this place was second only to London as a major trading port.

The quayside swarmed with hundreds of merchants, traders, porters, and seamen, all crowding its narrow streets and noisily going about their business, with none sparing a glance for him. Although bursting at the seams, Alec felt perversely safe here, just three unknown faces among a sea of strangers.

They had arrived late last evening after a brief stopover in Grantham, where they had lodged in a tavern overlooking the impressive stone carving of the second Eleanor Cross. The present king's grandfather, Edward—the first of that name—had ordered it built, one in a chain of twelve that stretched from Lincoln to Charing in London, each commemorating the place where his wife's coffin had rested on its final journey after her untimely death in Harby. In the years since Eleanor's passing, the crosses had become unofficial places of pilgrimage, with local residents happily catering to visitors from across the land. It was a touching tribute to Edward's love, one of the few monuments erected in his reign that wasn't an expression of his power and prestige.

After a hard journey that had taken them six days, Alec had been glad to ride into Boston little the worse for their travels. He had left Robert and Kit at the White Hart Inn while he made his way to the dock in search of the *Alexander McEwen* and its master, Captain William Grey.

He walked along the quay in the shadow of timber-framed warehouses and immense storage buildings, weaving through the industrious men thronging the wharves. Giant coils of rope were heaped beside the dock, alongside discarded packing crates and piles of wooden pallets, barrels of tar, and freshly hewn planking. The dockside appeared as a forest of masts, with the pennants of a dozen nations fluttering in the gentle breeze, and miles of taut rigging groaning in time to the gentle shift and swell of the river currents.

Halfway down the pier, Alec spotted his quarry, the single-mast *Alexander McEwen*, dwarfed by the tall ships crowding up against her wooden sides. She was a sturdy-looking vessel, sails neatly furled and stowed, hull recently retarred and shining black, with her gunports open, no doubt to air out the lower decks. Casting about briefly, Alec hurried up the gangplank and dropped onto her weathered deck, running immediately into a neatly dressed man he guessed was the captain.

"I'm a friend of James McEwen," he said, tipping his hat in respect.

"Captain William Grey," the man said, offering his hand. "Welcome aboard."

THE cabin was small but clean, with all the necessities stowed neatly on high shelves and nothing out of place. "It will be a bit of a tight squeeze," Grey said doubtfully.

He had quickly scanned the letter Alec had brought with him from Jamie, and was now rereading it more carefully as if to confirm its contents. "Three of you?" he asked, shaking his head. "I only hope you are friends."

Alec smiled. "We start the voyage that way," he said lightly. "It remains to be seen where we are at the end of ten days at sea."

Grey's mouth twitched as he returned his attention back to the letter. "Mr. McEwen tells me you are to decide at a later date whether you'll be making the return voyage. I'll have to ask you to advise me as soon as possible. We can always fill berths out of Bruges."

"Gladly," Alec agreed. "Much will depend on how we fare over the next few days."

Grey raised an eyebrow. "Are we to expect trouble?" he asked softly. "I'll not have my men blindsided."

"I would not bring my problems on board your ship, captain," Alec promised. "But I think it only fair to warn you that we are leaving the country for very good reason."

Grey looked at him intently for a long moment, then nodded. "As long as you don't endanger my crew, I won't pry into your business. But see that it is settled before you board my vessel, or at least that it stays on shore."

"When do we sail?" Alec asked.

"Three days hence on the morning tide," Grey replied.

Alec grimaced. He had been hoping for a quicker departure; three days seemed a long time to stay out of sight with so many enticements on their threshold.

"We have to wait for the last of the wool from Ludlow," Grey explained, reading his disappointment. "Most of it was floated by barge, but some of it is coming in on cart. It's a slower option, but it can't always be helped. We expect the last of it day after next, then we have to clear customs and pay our tax before we can load."

"I understand," Alec said, swallowing his anxiety. "We'll see you three days from now."

"Please don't be late," Captain Grey said. He waved the letter in his hand. "Mr. McEwen instructs us to sail without you if need be. It's beginning to look as though this might be the last shipment we make to Bruges. The king is threatening to embargo the Flemish ports to force their compliance with his French war."

"You must do as ordered, Captain," Alec said. "I consider myself duly warned." He shook Grey's hand and turned to leave, wondering whether it was possible to persuade Robert and Kit to lay low for three long days and nights with all the temptations that Boston had to offer.

"THE boy might need a nursemaid, but I have no intention of skulking here for the next three days," Robert said flatly.

"The 'boy' is eighteen years old and well able to look after himself," Kit retorted hotly, and Alec wished that he'd thought twice before suggesting that either of his friends hide themselves away until their ship was ready to sail.

"I'm only asking for caution," he said, throwing up a hand to stop any further protests. "I've already seen four City Guards patrolling the docks, though thankfully none were known to me. God alone knows how many people out there are connected to the League."

"Which is why I intend to take a room at a different inn," Robert said. It was his turn to throw up a staying hand as Alec opened his mouth to argue. "We draw too much attention to ourselves," Robert continued. "We don't know who is watching or how much they know, but they have likely been instructed to look out for three men traveling together, and the descriptions that were circulating around Cardeston were uncanny. If we stay together, we'll be easier to spot."

Alec nodded reluctantly. Even though the thought of splitting their group apart made him uneasy, Robert was right.

"Where will you go?" he asked.

"I'll find a place over on Albert Street," Robert said, naming a road that ran parallel to the quayside and contained a number of shabby boarding houses that catered mostly to foreign sailors. He picked up his saddlebag, which Alec only now noticed hadn't been unpacked, and slinging it over his shoulder, he crossed to the door.

"Can we at least agree to sup together?" Alec asked.

"Not tonight, Alec," Robert said. He made a slight gesture toward Kit. "We'll be penned together like cattle once we're on board. Let's take a few breaths alone while we have the chance."

Alec nodded again, hoping that the heat that flared through him didn't register on his face, although from the smile that Robert tried to hide, he doubted he had been that fortunate.

"Meet me on the quay tomorrow morning. We'll make our final arrangements," Robert said, before disappearing through the door and closing it behind him.

When Alec turned, he saw that Kit was trying not to laugh. "He's a remarkably skilled diplomat," he said sardonically.

Alec grimaced. "He means well," he said. "So, would you like to see something of Boston before supper?"

"I'd like that," Kit replied, his face lighting up. "I'd like it very much."

CONSTRUCTION on the church of St. Botolph's had been in progress for over twenty-five years, and it was well on its way to becoming the largest parish church in the land, but though impressive, Kit found the ordinary buildings that lined the quayside held more interest for him.

The huge warehouses of the German Hanse dominated the area, packed with wool from the Marches and the Fens, salt from the Lincolnshire coast, and lead from the mines of Derbyshire, all destined for the ports of Europe. In return, the Hanseatic merchants and their English counterparts imported finely woven cloth from Ghent and Douai, rich wine from Gascony, fish from Lubeck and

Bergen, timber and furs from the Baltic, and many of the spices that had made their way to Jamie McEwen's table.

The port teemed with fishermen and merchants from all those lands and more; in the space of an hour, Kit had heard the tongues of France, the Low Countries, Spain, and Italy as well as the many Germanic dialects of the Hanse, and seen the ships of over a dozen different trading nations anchored peaceably along the dock.

"It's impressive, isn't it?" Alec asked. Kit glanced at his friend and blushed when he saw the teasing smile that played on Alec's lips. Up until now, he had never seen this many people gathered in one place, and he knew that he must look slack-jawed with wonder.

"I can't believe that soon we will be a part of all this," he said. He stepped out of the way quickly as a line of carts trundled past, each heaped high with wooden crates and pushed by red-faced, muscular men. Even though it was past noon and the sun was high in the sky, the dockside was thrown into shadow by the tall warehouses, their large doors open wide to swallow up the merchandise that was being carted from the ships anchored along the waterfront.

Kit stopped as Alec grabbed at his sleeve. "There," Alec said, pointing down the quay. "The *Alexander McEwen*."

Kit spun around eagerly, though his heart sunk a little when he caught sight of the ship that they would soon be boarding. Although neat and trim, she seemed tiny in comparison to the mighty vessels that sat alongside her.

"She's a very fine boat," Alec said, reading his disappointment.

"I'm sure of it," Kit said quickly, not wanting to seem unappreciative.

Alec grinned. "She doesn't look like much when she's up against all those other vessels, but she's fleet and light. I'll bet she could outrun most of them if she had to."

Kit took a closer look and slowly nodded his agreement. After all, what they needed was something swift and agile, something that would carry them quickly down the River Witham and out into the Wash, then across the open sea to Flanders. "She's beautiful," he breathed, suddenly recognizing her most important attributes. "I wish we could board her sooner than three days' time."

"I'm not sure you'll be singing the same tune after a week living in Robert's pocket," Alec said dryly. "You'll likely be glad to be free of her."

Tugging at Kit's elbow, Alec led the way past the line of docked ships, making sure to keep to the shadows, his gaze darting from side to side as he assessed the men loitering in front of the warehouses. They had already steered clear of two members of the City Guard, easy enough to spot with the swan device embroidered on their surcoats. Kit kept his eyes open too, though it was a lot more difficult to judge who might be allied to the Sun League, given that they kept their markings hidden. Still, Kit felt the sunburst tattoo on his own chest tingle when he passed a particularly surly-looking man, or when he felt that somebody's eyes had fixed on him a shade too long for comfort. He was glad when Alec steered him into a small tavern sheltered beneath a tattered canvas awning, ducking his head to avoid the low lintel as he stepped into the gloomy interior.

They found a table tucked away in back, and soon they were enjoying a surprisingly delicious meat pie washed down with a pitcher of warm, dark beer.

"I hope Robert finds a meal half as good as this," Alec said, wiping crumbs from his chin.

"Does he mind?" Kit asked. "About us," he clarified when Alec looked momentarily confused. It seemed to Kit that Robert was unusually tolerant of his relationship with Alec, and unlike the men who had fawned over Marcus, Robert's feelings seemed genuine. Kit was used to men who were the picture of civility while Marcus was in the room, but who spat in his face as soon as their leader's back was turned. They called him filthy names, while accepting without question Marcus's right to fuck whomever he wanted. It was hard to believe that anybody could know what he had done, yet not regard him with revulsion, though he had never seen anything but compassion on Robert's face.

Alec was shaking his head. "I told you, Robert has the biggest heart of anybody I know. He has never condemned me, though he knows of my relationship with Jamie and my feelings for...." He stopped suddenly, glancing away, and Kit suspected that he wanted to say more, likely about the growing closeness between the two of them.

"But don't be misled," Alec continued, laughing. "That gruff exterior might hide a heart of gold, but Robert doesn't suffer fools gladly, and being on his wrong side is an uncomfortable place to find yourself."

"You've never been there, surely?" Kit protested.

Alec snorted. "More times than I care to recall," he said. "I had to work hard to prove myself. Sometimes I think I still haven't convinced him of my worth."

Kit didn't want to argue, but he felt sure that Alec underestimated how deep Robert's respect and affection for him ran. He looked across the table and into Alec's eyes, seeing something there he wasn't quite sure how to read.

"Did you ever...." Alec trailed off, then cleared his throat and began again. "Before de Crecy, was there anyone special?"

Kit shook his head mutely. He had thought there might be some spark with Alice Stone, a pretty redhead from the neighboring village. But his feelings for her had always been confused, and he had considered her more a sympathetic friend. They had fumbled their way to a kiss once or twice, though it was mostly out of curiosity on his part, and when Alice had gently rebuffed him, he hadn't pressed her for anything more. He had not known that men could lie together until Marcus had snatched him away from his home, and he had never felt anything but disgust in the man's bed, even when Marcus had been able to coax a response from his traitorous body.

"I don't know what there would have been for me if Marcus hadn't come along," Kit sighed. "Does it really matter?"

"I suppose not," Alec said, though there was something in his voice that made Kit think that he didn't believe the words even as he spoke them.

"You think I don't know my own mind," he said.

Alec shrugged, but he didn't deny Kit's observation.

"I've never felt this way before," Kit insisted.

"You've not had much opportunity," Alec reminded gently.

Kit shook his head. "I'd feel this way if I'd had all the experience in the world," he said firmly.

Alec smiled, but there was a trace of sadness in his eyes. "I hope we get the chance to test that conviction," he said. "But you must allow the possibility that your feelings will change when you are free to make your own choices. I'd not see you mistake gratitude for something more profound." Alec glanced away briefly, and when he looked back, there was new resolve in his eyes. "And I'd not stand in your way should you decide to explore other options."

Out of respect for Alec's concern, Kit refrained from pursuing the point further, but the swell of his heart made him more certain than ever before: he had fallen in love with Alec Weston.

THE quayside was still bustling with activity when they stepped back into the fading sunlight. Kit's head was swimming with the aftereffects of the strong, locally brewed beer, the second pitcher having gone down as easily as the first. He suspected he had drunk more of it than Alec, who was following close behind, steadier on his feet than Kit.

He scanned the immediate area as they left the tavern. The constant ebb and flow of people confused him momentarily, until the fresh air cleared his head and he was able to focus on his surroundings. At first all seemed as it should be; then, out of the corner of his eye, he spotted a bearded man lounging against the tavern wall, who straightened quickly when he caught sight of them. Kit turned his head a fraction, and his blood ran cold when the man discreetly brushed his right hand over his heart, his thumb and forefinger making the shape of a circle, signaling that he was a member of the Sun League.

With his heart thudding against his ribcage, Kit opened his mouth to warn Alec, but the words froze on his tongue when he spied another man silently appearing from the shadow of a laneway and flashing the same sign in Kit's direction. He swallowed loudly, hurrying to keep up with Alec's long strides as they quickly made their way back to the inn. By the time they reached the tavern on Church Street, Kit had seen two further League signs, and realized that he and Alec were completely surrounded.

It was only when they were in sight of the inn that Kit understood why the men who were following them had not pounced: standing in front of the building, bundled in a great black cloak, was the unmistakable silhouette of Stephen Brody, one of Marcus de Crecy's most trusted allies.

Alec was too intent on hurrying them back to the inn to notice the man he had briefly encountered once before, but Kit recognized him immediately. He cast around quickly, realizing with a jolt that it was too late to change course. As they drew closer, Stephen locked eyes with Kit, then flashed him a different hand signal, this one indicating a question. Though Kit was sick with apprehension, he had the presence of mind to form a quick succession of gestures that instructed Stephen to hold his position. Stephen had been the closest thing to a friend during the painful years Kit had spent with the Sun League, and though he didn't expect much consideration, he prayed that Stephen would at least grant him a few moments alone with Alec, even if only out of surprise at the request. Stephen's eyes widened momentarily and he took a half step closer, but in the end he nodded briefly and allowed Kit and Alec to pass unmolested.

Kit breathed out a deep sigh of relief when he and Alec gained the relative safety of their room, though he knew it was nothing more than a temporary reprieve. He threw off his cloak, crossed to the narrow window, and peered through a gap in the wooden shutters onto the road below. Stephen was still standing outside, his face turned upward, eyes fixed on the window, and around him stood the men of the Sun League, waiting to receive his instructions.

Kit's heart clenched painfully; mere hours ago the bright dream of freedom had been so close that he could almost touch it. Now it evaporated, leaving only emptiness and a deep dread.

"You're very quiet." Alec's voice startled him, and he turned abruptly to face his friend, who was watching him quizzically from across the room.

"Too much to drink," Kit said, only half lying; his head was pounding, and his mouth felt as though it was full of ash.

Alec winced in sympathy. "Let me fetch you some water," he offered.

"I'll go," Kit said quickly. Stephen had shown remarkable restraint, but Kit knew it wouldn't be long before he was banging at the door demanding answers.

"It's no trouble," Alec insisted.

Kit crossed the room and stroked Alec's stubbled cheek. "I need the air," he said softly.

Alec smiled and Kit's heart leapt. Depending on Stephen's mood, this might be the last time he would see Alec Weston. He buried both hands in Alec's hair and pulled him close, pressing their mouths together in an urgent kiss. When he pulled back, Alec was flushed and a little breathless.

"Hurry back," he urged.

Kit dropped his hands and stepped away, afraid that if he didn't, he would never let go. "I'll be back as soon as I can," he promised, then turned and hurried out. Stephen had come back into the inn and was only yards from the door, pacing up and down the hallway. His eyes narrowed speculatively when he saw Kit. "It's good to see you, boy," he murmured.

Kit was unable to reply, his voice seemingly stuck in his parched throat. He tugged at Stephen's sleeve, pulling him into the dark recess of an open doorway.

"Marcus will be pleased we found you at last," Stephen said.

The implication loosened whatever had strangled the words in Kit's mouth. "He's here?" he choked out, glad that his voice was reasonably steady even as his heart pounded loudly.

"He's close enough," Stephen replied.

"How did you find me?" Kit asked.

"Friends in low places," Stephen replied, grinning widely. "Come now! You've not been away so long you've forgotten how many people pocket our coin. We lost sight of you when you left Shrewsbury, but we picked up your trail again out of Ludlow, and Marcus wouldn't give us a moment's peace until we'd tracked you all the way across the country. You certainly led us a merry dance."

Kit felt his chest tighten as Stephen frowned. "We thought you were being taken to the Lord Chancellor in London, but then we heard that the Guard was hunting you too. What's going on, Kit?"

"It's a long story," Kit said.

"Get your things together then," Stephen continued. "I'll deal with the Guardsman inside."

Kit clutched fearfully at Stephen's arm. "You've misunderstood," he said urgently. "He defied the Lord Chancellor in order to save my life. It's why the City Guard is hunting him."

Uncertainty flared briefly in Stephen's eyes; then he shrugged. "It's for Marcus to decide what to do."

The pain in Kit's chest intensified until it felt as though his heart would burst. He couldn't allow Marcus to lay hands on either Alec or Robert, nor could he let his friends continue to fight what was fast becoming a hopeless battle. The Sun League's noose was tightening relentlessly around them, and Alec and Robert's dreadful fate seemed all but sealed. Still, Kit thought he saw a faint glimmer of hope. Though it shattered his bright dream into a thousand pieces and struck terror into his soul, he summoned all his courage. "You know him, Stephen. Marcus will strike before the Guardsman has a chance to defend himself. Give me time to talk to Marcus before you bring the Guardsman in. I'll accompany you now and plead his case."

"I don't know about that," Stephen said doubtfully.

"You'll lose nothing by it." Kit pleaded. "If Marcus wants him, you know where to find him."

Stephen inclined his head, his eyes searching Kit's face, but in the end he nodded slowly. "On your head be it," he said. "Come. We'll leave as soon as it gets light."

Kit bit his lip, frantically searching for a reason that would persuade Stephen to let him return to the room. He wanted to try to warn Alec, though he knew he would have to find a way to do it without revealing the details of the plan his friend would never countenance, and he desperately wanted to see Alec one last time. "Captain Weston saved my life," he blurted. "Would you give me leave to say my farewells?"

He tried to school his expression to hide his turbulent emotions. "We can't travel in the dark," he said, hoping to appeal to Stephen's common sense.

Stephen frowned as he considered the options. "I suppose that would do no harm," he said reluctantly. He leaned closer and murmured, "My men have the place surrounded. If you're not here by daybreak, I'll kick the door down and bury my sword in that Guardsman's gut, whether he saved your life or not."

"He's leaving early," Kit promised. "Let him pass unharmed, and we'll be on our way."

He turned, but Stephen grasped his wrist and held him fast. "And you swear you'll not play me false, Kit?" he said softly, his eyes boring into Kit's own.

Kit placed his hand over the fingers tightening painfully around him. "I swear it on my life," he promised.

Stephen released him suddenly. "That would certainly be the price you'd have to pay," he warned.

"WHERE'S the water?" Alec asked, amusement dancing in his eyes.

"I was so thirsty I finished it on the way," Kit said.

"Are you feeling better?"

Kit nodded, not trusting himself to speak. Alec smiled and bent to stir the dying embers in the grate. The warm light danced across his flushed skin, making his blue eyes shine. When he straightened, he glanced at Kit, looking uncharacteristically uncertain.

Without speaking, Kit undid the lacings of his doublet and dropped it onto the floor, then tugged his shirt over his head, baring his torso. A moment later Alec held out his hand, and the simplicity of the gesture caught at Kit's heart, making it race. He moved across the room and reached out to slip his palm into the outstretched hand.

His whole body tingled as Alec brushed gentle lips against the side of his face. Alec wrapped his arms around Kit, lightly tracing the raised lines on Kit's back, and Kit shuddered, wondering briefly how many more stripes would soon accompany the mass that already marred him. He breathed in deeply, smelling the smoke from the fire that clung to Alec's hair, feeling the muscled body shudder against his own. Alec shifted slightly and the hardness between his legs brushed against Kit's own lengthening prick. He sucked in a sharp breath and pulled Alec closer, pressing their mouths together for a deep kiss.

When Alec drew away and tugged him down onto the bed, he went unresistingly and rolled on top of his friend, feeling warm skin against his own. Alec's bright eyes locked with his, and Kit cupped a hand to his friend's cheek, sweeping his thumb over soft lips and feeling a tingle when Alec's tongue darted out and dampened the callused pad.

It was hard to accept that it all ended here; that after the tentative journey to find their way to each other, they would have so little time together.

"What's troubling you?"

Kit started, realizing that he was in danger of betraying himself. "I'm glad I met you," he whispered.

"You're glad I arrested you?" Alec said wryly. "Glad I almost got you hanged?"

"Meeting you was the best thing that has ever happened to me," Kit said, meaning it from the bottom of his heart.

Alec cocked his head, studying Kit closely. "You're very solemn tonight."

It took an enormous effort, but Kit managed to muster a smile. "Promise me one thing?" he asked.

"Anything," Alec said.

"Promise you'll not take foolish risks if things do not work out as planned."

Alec frowned. "What do you mean?" he asked.

"You know what I mean," Kit said quietly. "The place is swarming with City Guards, and it's only a matter of time before the League catches up with us." He suppressed a shudder at the thought of Stephen Brody, mere steps away, with his men ranged close about. "If things don't work out, I want you to recognize the end when you see it. I want you to accept whatever fate has been written for us."

Alec took Kit's hand and placed it over the scars on his chest, then lightly traced the markings on Kit's back. "I thought our fates were now intertwined," he said softly.

Though the words gladdened Kit, they also sent a leaden chill through his limbs. In his heart he knew it was unlikely that he could convince Marcus to let Alec and Robert go; the only real alternative was that he could buy some time so his friends could slip the net that was closing around them. They were both seasoned campaigners, and Kit clung to the hope that, when they found he was missing, they would realize what was happening and would take steps to save themselves.

While it was unlikely Alec would tamely accept Kit's return to Marcus after they had fought so hard for his freedom, Kit prayed that his friend was sensible enough to bow to the inevitable in the face of the Sun League's overwhelming presence. If not, he counted on Robert's pragmatism to prevail, hoping he would force Alec to accept reality and move on, no matter how much he railed.

Alec must have read something of his despair, because the next thing Kit knew, he had been flipped onto his back and Alec was hovering over him, bemusement clear in his deep blue eyes.

"You are a very maudlin drunk," Alec said. "But if it makes you feel better, I promise to accept what is written in the stars!"

"Thank you," Kit said, ignoring Alec's flippant tone and feeling a weight lift off him. He knew he could face whatever hardship tomorrow would bring, as long as it safeguarded the lives of his friends. He looked up into Alec's face; in his darkest hours, he would conjure up this beautiful smile, and every fresh welt, every hurt, every humiliation would be that much easier to bear.

He let his hands roam over Alec's muscled body, mapping every inch; he buried his face against warm skin that smelled faintly of leather and smoke, and breathed deeply; he watched the changing expressions on his lover's face, trying to commit them all to memory. And when Alec gently eased inside him, filling him with desperate joy, he rode the wave of passion that seared through every limb, clinging tightly long after Alec had fallen into sated sleep.

As the waning moon poured milky light through the slats of the shutters, Kit watched the shallow rise and fall of Alec's every breath and the sweet innocence that stole across his relaxed features, until the light began to warm and yellow as the sun rose. His own breath caught when Alec's eyes fluttered open and met his, and a brittle laugh escaped him when Alec tumbled him down onto the straw-filled mattress and kissed him sleepily. It took everything he had to let Alec go, to watch him stand up and cover his lithe body with clothing, all the while chatting casually about his plans for the day.

When he was ready, he grabbed up his cloak and strode to the door, then turned to smile at Kit. "I should be no more than an hour," he said. "Robert wants a quick word with Captain Grey. I'll bring him back with me, and we can breakfast together."

Kit nodded, unable to speak.

Alec's smile deepened and his bright eyes twinkled. "Why don't you get some more sleep?" he said kindly. "You still look a little worse for wear." He turned to leave.

"Alec!"

Alec turned back and looked at him expectantly.

There was so much to say: remembrances and promises, gratitude and wonder, and above all, love. But in the end, words failed. "Whatever happens, remember that you changed my life," he said simply, because nothing else seemed fitting.

Alec's calm expression faltered, and Kit had to force himself to smile. "Take care," he said, resisting the overwhelming urge to leap out of bed and take Alec back into his arms. Stephen was likely already hovering outside the door, and he couldn't risk delaying Alec's departure any longer.

"I'll see you soon," Alec said. He raised his hand in a parting salute, then disappeared.

An iciness stole over Kit, draining all warmth and feeling and weaving a tight grip around his heart, so that when the latch on the door rose and Stephen stepped into the room, he felt emptied of all emotion.

"Come, Kit," Stephen said, beckoning with a gloved hand. "Marcus is waiting."

THEY rode north along a dirt track, Stephen flanking him closely, his men boxing Kit in on all sides. The sun was shining brightly, and the air was filled with the fragrance of flowers and the music of birdsong; if not for the knowledge of what was waiting for him at the end of the journey, it would have been a perfect spring day.

"Not far now," Stephen said. "You'll have to bear up for a couple of days—Marcus will have some questions. Then we can put all this behind us and return home."

Kit winced, his imagination painting a graphic picture of what he'd face before they could all move on. He couldn't help noticing how Stephen looked away quickly, well aware of Marcus's present mood. It was so achingly familiar; he wondered fleetingly if he had ever really believed that escape was possible or if he'd always known, somewhere deep in the corners of his heart, that Marcus would find him again.

"And the Guardsman?" he asked haltingly. If he had bought Alec a fighting chance, then anything would be worth bearing.

Stephen shrugged. "As you wanted, he is unharmed."

Ten minutes later they rounded a turn, and he saw Stephen straighten in his saddle and knew that they had arrived. Up ahead a ramshackle inn squatted by the roadside under the branches of a spreading chestnut tree. Several armed men ringed the building, their arrows casually aimed at his heart, but they did nothing more than follow his progress as he drew near. Kit shivered as they plodded into a shaded courtyard, though he doubted it had anything to do with the sudden coolness in temperature and more to do with the man filling the doorway, his dark eyes fixed on Kit's face.

Stephen leapt off his mount and crossed the two steps to Kit's horse. He caught at the stirrup and looked up, his features tight with apprehension. "Whatever happens, remember that he still wants you. He wouldn't have come all this way otherwise. He'd have just sent me to finish you off."

Kit nodded mutely, wondering whether the words were meant to provide comfort. He kicked out of the stirrups, swung his leg over his mount, and slid off and onto the ground. He was glad he was holding tightly to the horn of his saddle when his legs buckled, though he righted himself quickly enough and stood up straight. Although his blood was pounding against his temples, he forced himself to hold Marcus's gaze as he walked toward the doorway, deliberately stopping several paces away.

"Marcus," he croaked, his throat dry and raw.

Marcus's hungry eyes swept him slowly from top to bottom. He crooked his finger, and Kit summoned all of his courage and dragged his leaden legs forward until he was standing directly in front of Marcus.

"I missed you," Marcus said, so softly that Kit wasn't sure he'd heard right. Marcus raised his hand slowly and slid it behind Kit's neck. He tugged until Kit was flush up against his body, feeling the strain of hard muscles and the bulging prick that pressed against his groin. Marcus leaned in and kissed him, his dry lips tasting of wine, his tongue pushing insistently into Kit's mouth as his other hand slid around Kit's back to knead the muscles of his backside.

Marcus deepened the kiss, tightening his hand in Kit's hair while his hips thrust forward, driving his hardness against Kit's body. With a sharp tug, he pulled Kit's head back and sucked at his neck, his teeth scraping so hard along the column of Kit's throat that Kit couldn't contain a small gasp. Marcus raised his head, his eyes heavy with lust, and before Kit could register the change in mood, Marcus slapped him hard across the mouth, making him stumble backward and fall to the ground.

"Where the hell have you been?" Marcus growled.

Turning his head, Kit spat a mouthful of blood into the dirt, then slowly climbed to his feet to face the man who once again owned his life.

CHAPTER 11

IT WAS uncomfortably warm in the small hall that served as the inn's dining room, though Kit couldn't be sure that the sweat trickling down his spine wasn't caused by the horror of being back in Marcus de Crecy's hands.

Marcus had flung his arm around Kit's shoulders in an unnervingly affable way and guided him into the inn as though they were old friends about to get reacquainted after a long absence. His men had stepped back quickly as they passed, watching Kit with a mixture of relief and unmistakable pity on their faces, and it was clear that though they had little use for him, most were glad to see Kit back by their leader's side.

Marcus dropped his arm and sat at a table on which plates of food were piled high, and he began eating while he grilled Kit relentlessly on the events of the past weeks. Kit stood beside the table, and when Marcus picked up a mug and gestured wordlessly, Kit located a pitcher of wine and dutifully poured a generous measure.

Marcus grunted his thanks, then tore into a capon while he kept his eyes on Kit's face, watching him thoughtfully.

"So, you did not betray us to the Lord Chancellor when you were taken," he said, breaking the tense silence that had fallen.

"No, sir," Kit replied.

"Though doubtless you were cajoled," Marcus continued. "What was the threat?"

Kit shrugged. "That I'd be hung," he said quietly, shivering at the memory. A murmur ran through the men gathered in the room, though at a curt gesture from Marcus, they quieted.

"And what did he offer you for your cooperation?" Marcus pressed.

"Protection," Kit said, "for myself and my family."

Marcus snorted. "I take it you didn't believe him?" he said dryly.

"I know better," Kit replied. He leaned in and refilled the rapidly emptying cup, spilling a little wine when Marcus grabbed his wrist.

"And you would have swung for us?" he murmured. "You would not have thought to take the offer?"

Kit met his eyes steadily. "You tried to kill me, Marcus," he said softly. "You may assume I knew you were serious."

Marcus barked out a laugh and let him go. He tore off a hunk of bread and dipped it into a steaming bowl before cramming it into his mouth and chewing loudly. "And these men who took you," he said, making the hair on the back of Kit's neck stand on end. "You say they helped you escape the Lord Chancellor?"

Kit nodded, not trusting himself to speak. Marcus's eyes returned to his face, boring into him with what felt like a physical pressure.

"They are City Guard. Why would they help you?" Marcus demanded.

Kit licked his lips. "They are men of honor, sir," he said. "They would not see me hang just because I refused to betray you."

"And where are they now, these honorable men?" Marcus asked, sarcasm lacing his words.

Kit pulled in a deep breath as Stephen darted a glance at him. "I asked Stephen to let them go," he said.

Marcus's jaw tightened. "By what authority did you think to do that?" he asked, dangerously quiet.

"They saved my life, Marcus," Kit said, his voice shaking slightly, despite his best efforts. "They sacrificed their livelihoods and their position in the Guard to help me. I thought to show them mercy."

"Mercy!" Marcus thundered, slamming his hand down on the wooden table and making the dishes rattle. "You would have these men make a fool of me? They took what belongs to me. There will be no mercy!" His voice had risen, and his face was flushed deep red with anger. Kit could feel his legs beginning to tremble; it was clear that Marcus was not to be persuaded to clemency. He felt a rush of pure relief that Stephen had agreed to let Alec go.

Stephen shuffled his feet, and there was something in his expression that suddenly made Kit's flesh crawl. "Do you want me to pick them up?" Stephen asked.

Kit flinched at the words, and his eyes cut back quickly to Marcus, who was watching him closely.

"The *Alexander McEwen*," Marcus said distinctly. "That's the name of the ship, is it not?"

Kit felt his growing apprehension transform into abject fear. "How could you know that?" he stammered, swiveling his head wildly between Marcus and Stephen.

"Do you take us for fools?" Marcus roared. "We've known your plans since you left Ludlow."

"We've been waiting here for several days, Kit," Stephen said, sounding almost apologetic. "We've had eyes on you ever since you arrived."

Kit could scarcely believe his ears. While he and his friends had ducked and weaved through back roads and rural tracks, jumping at every shadow, the Sun League had simply strolled into Boston and lain in wait for them.

"How?" he asked, hardly able to form the question.

"Your Captain Weston should take more care of those he counts as friends," Marcus sneered. "They can be a treacherous bunch of bastards."

It was hard to take in what Marcus was saying; the implication of treachery was so terrible.

"We've been waiting for the best opportunity to separate you from your protectors," Stephen said. "We thought it likely you'd come home more willingly without them around."

Kit's eyes widened in horror, and he turned toward Marcus, cringing at the look of satisfaction on his face.

"You still have them under watch?" Marcus said, addressing Stephen but keeping his eyes trained on Kit.

"Aye," Stephen confirmed. "We haven't let them out of our sight." Kit hissed in a sharp breath, and Stephen's gaze slid away from him. Stephen had clearly lied when he'd promised to let Alec go. Though Kit couldn't say that his duplicity was wholly unexpected, he had always thought of Stephen as a friend, and the outright betrayal was painful to swallow.

"Then you know what must be done," Marcus ordered.

A wave of hopeless despair washed through Kit, its bitterness all but overwhelming him. Marcus would doubtless make him suffer, but he would survive, while Alec and Robert would be executed simply because they had allowed themselves to be moved by his plight. The injustice burned in him, hot as a forge fire, and with it an image of his proud, principled friends, destroyed by Marcus de Crecy's lust for vengeance. Without thinking, he took a step forward and grabbed Marcus's sleeve.

"Please, Marcus," he pleaded. "I beg you to spare their lives. If I mean anything to you, please grant this request."

Marcus's lips thinned and his eyes glittered dangerously. "What makes you think you are in a position to ask anything of me?" he hissed. He shook Kit's hand off and lashed out, and for the second time, Kit found himself sprawled on the floor, his mouth filled with the iron tang of blood.

"They saved you from the Lord Chancellor's noose," Marcus said. "But you did not return to us. Did they force you to accompany them here?"

Though he knew it would cost him dearly, Kit did not hesitate; he could not bear to think of Robert and Alec falsely accused. "No, sir," he said clearly. "I traveled freely and of my own accord."

The high color that had flooded Marcus's face ebbed, leaving a blank stillness. Kit knew that this controlled rage was more dangerous than Marcus's sudden fiery outbursts, and despite his best efforts, he could no longer hide his fear.

Without turning his head, Marcus held out a hand, and Stephen slapped a short-handled whip into his palm.

"I thought you learned your lesson last time you ran," Marcus said. "But it seems you are a dull pupil." He turned back toward Stephen. "I want those Guards taken care of before the day is out," he snapped.

"As you wish," Stephen said. He turned, gathered the rest of the men, and hurried out of the room while throwing a final remorseful look at Kit.

It was only when a sharp pain cut across the back of his hand that Kit realized Marcus had moved and was looming over him, trailing the bloodied whip.

"Nobody takes what's mine," he growled.

With startling strength, he hauled Kit to his feet, spun him around, and slammed him down onto the table. The side of Kit's face slid through a puddle of spilled wine, his skin burning as the coarse wood tore at his cheek. He stiffened as Marcus ripped his shirt in two.

"You want to know what you mean to me?"

Kit gasped as the lash came down hard across his back.

"Let me show you," Marcus growled.

"I DON'T have to ask whether you had a good night!"

Alec smiled at Robert's sardonic observation, although he didn't think it deserved a response. He felt a hot blush rise up to flood his cheeks, wondering at Robert's continuing ability to discomfit.

"How was your evening?" he asked.

"Likely not as sweet as yours," Robert grumbled. "I was abroad, getting the lay of the land."

"And?" Alec prompted.

"And there are an awful lot of ruffians about," Robert said.

Alec caught his elbow and steered him along the wooden planking that ran beside the quay. "Anybody we should be worried about?" he murmured, his eyes unconsciously darting left and right.

Robert shot him a sidelong look. "A good half dozen I'd not care to meet on a dark night," he said dryly.

Alec swore under his breath, then sidestepped quickly as a group of men staggered across his path, weighed down with sacks they'd hefted onto their shoulders. As he stepped aside, pulling Robert with him, he caught a glimpse of two dark eyes following his movements.

"We have company," he murmured into Robert's ear.

"Black cape, scar on his right cheek," Robert replied. "He's been practically stepping in your shadow since you arrived." He continued walking forward, Alec hurrying to keep abreast of him. "Mine's making a better job of it," Robert said softly. "Green doublet over my left shoulder."

Alec resisted the urge to turn around and stare.

"League?" he breathed.

Robert shrugged. "Let's find out."

They weaved quickly in and out of the men crowding the dock, until Robert made a sharp left turn that brought them into one of the narrow streets that threaded between the warehouses. Darting into a doorway, they hung back in the shadows, daggers drawn, until the follower with the green doublet had hurried past; seconds later they heard the heavy footfalls of the second man. They waited until he had drawn level with their hiding place, then Robert jumped out and covered the startled man's mouth with his gloved hand, pulling him off balance and dragging him into the doorway. Alec slammed him up against the wall, relishing the moment of surprise that flared in his dark eyes before his expression turned hard and blank.

"Who are you?" Alec growled.

The man didn't move. Alec raised his dagger to the man's throat, but he didn't so much as blink. Exchanging a quick glance with Robert, Alec used his dagger to slice through the man's tunic and shirt, ripping the material apart. His blood turned to ice in his veins when he saw the distinctive tattoo emblazoned over the man's heart, the sunburst that marked him as a member of the Sun League.

"Sweet Jesus," he murmured. He turned his head and flinched at the grim expression on Robert's face. "Kit," he gasped.

Without a word, Robert drove the heel of his hand hard under the chin of the outlaw, snapping his head back against the wall with a loud crack. The man looked stunned for a moment, then his legs gave out, and he crumpled into an ungainly heap on the ground.

"We don't have much time," Robert said. "If they spotted us, they'll be watching Kit too."

"God, I was a fool to leave him alone," Alec hissed.

"No time for that now," Robert snapped. "Let's go."

He turned on his heel and strode off, with Alec barely half a step behind him.

"THE young gentleman rode out less than an hour ago," the boy said. "The innkeeper saw him talking to a man, then he just left."

His pulse racing, Alec nodded and handed the boy a groat. He and Robert had sprinted as fast as they could, but it appeared as though they were too late; the inn was surrounded by shifty-looking strangers who were too avidly focused on the surroundings to be innocent passersby, and there was no sign of Kit.

Robert had hailed a young boy on the street and sent him into the inn with instructions to glean information on Kit and his whereabouts without betraying his actions to the watching men. The boy had been gone so long Alec had begun to fear he had been found out, but just when he was about to give up, the lad sauntered out of the inn and crossed the street to where he and Robert were hiding in a shadowy side street.

The young boy's eyes gleamed greedily as he closed his hand around the coin. "The innkeeper said he'll tell you in which direction your friend headed as soon as you pay him what you owe," he said solemnly.

Robert snorted in disgust, but Alec simply shrugged and fetched another coin from his belt. He held it out, and the young boy snatched at it and darted away. Halfway across the road, he skidded to a halt and turned. "They went north," he shouted, then turned again and took to his heels, running in the opposite direction, away from the inn.

"Thieving little bastard," Robert snarled, surging forward. Alec grabbed his arm and held him back.

"Let it go," he barked.

"How can you be sure of anything he said?" Robert demanded.

"He didn't need to tell us which direction they took," Alec pointed out. "I see no gain to him in lying about that. He already had the money."

"I suppose so," Robert agreed reluctantly. "I wonder how long before the Sun League recruit him," he muttered sourly.

Alec turned back toward the inn, his eyes searching out any clues, but he didn't recognize any of the men loitering outside the doorway, and there was nothing to indicate who they were. Still, the two men who had shadowed him and Robert, and the sick feeling in the pit of his stomach, were enough to convince him that Kit had been taken by the Sun League.

"They have him, Robert," he murmured. "I'm sure of it."

Robert eyed him thoughtfully before nodding. "Aye, I believe you are right," he sighed. "Let me ask around, see if I can find out where they are heading—"

"You won't have to do that," Alec interrupted.

"Why not?" Robert asked, frowning.

Alec turned to face him and looked directly into his friend's eyes. He didn't say anything, but Robert knew him well enough, and clearly read the resolve on his face. Robert's mouth tightened and his frown intensified, creasing his brow in a deep furrow. "I'm not going to let you do anything stupid, Alec," he said firmly.

"De Crecy has him," Alec said simply. "You know what that animal will do."

"You'll be no use to the boy if you do anything reckless," Robert insisted. "We'll figure something out, and we'll stand together, as always."

Alec clapped a hand on his friend's shoulder. "I told you once before that you were not obliged to travel this path with me," he said. Robert opened his mouth, no doubt to protest, but Alec squeezed his shoulder, demanding his attention. "This time I'm not asking," he said, his voice quiet but resolute. "You've already risked your livelihood and been forced to leave your home. I'll not have the next step on my conscience. This is the end of the road, my friend. I can't share the rest of the way with you."

Robert's eyes glittered, and underneath Alec's hand, his body stiffened with tension. "What would you have me do? Abandon you when you are most in need of good counsel?"

Alec ignored the jibe. "Go back to Ludlow. I've left instructions with Jamie. You'll be well provided for...."

"I'm being bought off?" Robert scoffed.

Alec didn't want their last encounter to end in bitterness and recrimination, but neither did he have the time to consider Robert's feelings. "Jamie is holding enough funds to buy your commission back in the City Guard. Even now he's greasing the right palms to make your return easier."

Robert shrugged his hand off, anger clear to read on his weathered face. "You knew something like this would happen," he accused.

Alec looked away, unable to deny it. "We're old campaigners," he said instead. "We know the risks. We prepare for the worst."

He wasn't prepared, however, when Robert slammed him up against the hard stone wall, all but knocking the breath out of him. His hands bunched in Alec's tunic, holding him fast, and his red face hovered just inches away from Alec's own. "Listen carefully, I'll say this but once," he growled. "I am not going to let you risk your foolish neck attempting the impossible to achieve absolutely nothing!"

Alec relaxed against the iron grip, knowing that it was useless to struggle. "Is that what you told yourself," he whispered, "when you set out alone to rescue me from the Sun League three years ago?"

Anger flared on Robert's face; then he released Alec suddenly. "That's a low blow and you know it," he said, scowling fiercely.

Alec smoothed the front of his tunic. "I'm sorry," he said softly, looking directly into Robert's stormy eyes. "I don't have any choice. I don't think I can let him go."

"Did I say anything about letting him go?" Robert growled. "What I said is that you're not going to do anything stupid. Not by yourself anyway. And if you so much as consider that suggestion again, I'll stick my boot so far up your arse you'll be tasting leather for weeks. Do I make myself clear, Captain Weston?"

Alec grinned, silently acknowledging the huge sense of relief that Robert had chosen to stay with him. "I think that was plain enough, Robert," he quipped. He sobered quickly and clasped Robert's hand in his. "Thank you, my friend," he said fervently.

"You'd just make a dog's breakfast of it," Robert grumbled. "Now, what's the plan?"

Alec winced. "I was going to offer to trade my life for his," he admitted.

Robert stared, his mouth opening and closing, though no words came out. "That was the plan?" he finally asked, incredulously. "The whole plan?"

Alec nodded sheepishly.

"By God, you're stupider than I thought," Robert snorted. He held up a hand when Alec opened his mouth to defend himself. "Not another word," he admonished. "Give me a minute to think this through. Let's see if we can't improve a little on your brilliant strategy."

KIT shivered in the cool air as he struggled to his feet and stepped out of the shallow tin bath, tepid water sloshing over the rim and soaking the rushes that covered the packed-earth floor. The soapy water had soothed his torn skin and cleaned away the sticky blood, though it had done nothing to dull the searing pain.

He winced as he pulled on a shirt, wondering how much worse he looked with a fresh set of whip marks covering his back. Groaning out loud, he struggled into his breeches, the fine wool rubbing against the stripes cut into his backside. Marcus had not spared the rod, and the free-flowing blood had soaked through his tattered clothing and dripped onto the dirt floor. When Marcus had finished, he had ordered Kit to clean himself up, and Kit had not dared to look into the man's face as he'd stumbled out of the room and into the chamber adjoining the hall.

He warily eyed a beautifully worked satin doublet, setting it aside when he decided that it would chafe his raw skin too badly. It had been a shock to find that Marcus had brought this clothing along with him, so certain of his ability to recapture Kit. His spirit had shriveled when he opened the chest filled with the sumptuous garments Marcus liked to see him wear, yet another symbol of the man's absolute control over him.

Kit sighed deeply, wondering when he could safely seek out Tom Riley, one of Marcus's men skilled in the art of the apothecary, who could brew up a potion that took the edge off pain, even as it slowed the wits and induced sleep. Marcus was not averse to him taking the draft, although he usually made sure Kit had suffered adequately before he allowed it.

Kit limped painfully to the window and threw open the rotting wooden shutters to gaze out into the inn's shady courtyard. It was filled with men milling about idly, all waiting for Marcus to give the signal to move on. The thought of the journey made Kit's heart sink; it would truly signal the end of his dream of a new life. He was already heartsick that Alec and Robert had given up so much for him, only to fail at the last. He tried to take comfort in the keen hope that they would be able to evade Stephen's men and escape with their lives, but as time passed with no further word, it was becoming increasingly difficult to maintain faith.

He jumped when the door opened, but forced himself to straighten when Marcus walked in.

"Take a good look," Marcus said. "It will be a long time before you see the light of day again."

Resigned as he was to Marcus's threats, Kit felt his gut cramp at the prospect of being indefinitely confined to camp. The endless hours of boredom were made worse by the casual contempt of Marcus's followers, most of whom avoided or ignored Kit, afraid that he would tattle to their leader, though he had never spoken a word against any of them. At least when he was taking part in the business of the League he was relatively free to roam, though he was always conscious of the invisible leash that tethered him.

Marcus beckoned, and Kit crossed the floor warily, heaving a great sigh of relief when Marcus simply gestured to a trunk. Kit pulled out a clean shirt and laid it on the bed, then began to undo the lacings of Marcus's doublet, his fingers clumsy at first, then falling easily back into old habits.

"What happened to your hair?" Marcus asked, eyeing him curiously.

"It was getting in my way, so I cut it off," Kit replied.

"I don't like it. Let it grow back," Marcus ordered.

"Yes, Marcus," Kit sighed. He eased the doublet off and helped Marcus out of his shirt, trying not to look too closely at his own blood spattering the sleeve. Marcus slipped the clean shirt over his head, then held out his arms as Kit pulled the doublet back on and began to lace it up.

"Your mother told me you came to see her," Marcus said.

Kit stiffened. "You saw her?" he asked.

"I paid her a special visit," Marcus replied, his dark eyes flashing. "She could not tell me where you were going, but she described your companion well enough. What is he like, this Captain Weston?"

Kit shrugged, trying to keep his expression neutral. "As I said, a man of honor."

"You threw your lot in with him quickly enough," Marcus mused. "There must have been some good reason."

"There was reason enough," Kit retorted. "You loosed an arrow at my heart and only failed to kill me because Captain Weston pulled me out of harm's way."

Marcus waved a dismissive hand. "I could not risk you betraying the League, and I knew you'd be sorely pressed by the Lord Chancellor."

"I kept faith," Kit insisted. "And yet I am punished—"

"You know the way it is as well as anybody," Marcus interrupted. "Your mother certainly knew. She was easily persuaded to tell me what I wanted to know."

"Did you hurt her?" Kit said tightly.

"Don't be a fool," Marcus snapped. "She is under my protection now. She understands well where her allegiance lies."

Kit could have laughed out loud at the irony. He had been willing to hang to protect his mother, and all the while she had allied herself to the man who had kidnapped her son. He shook his head, trying to be fair; she had been left alone with two children to raise, and he could not blame her for taking what must have seemed the only path open to her.

"Why did you not tell me my mother had remarried?" Kit asked. "I had a right to know."

"Perhaps if you learned to behave yourself, you would earn such considerations," Marcus said. "But you continually find new ways to infuriate me."

"It is not such a difficult thing to do," Kit muttered, though he regretted his insolence when Marcus's eyebrows drew together in a formidable frown. Luckily Marcus was distracted when the door opened and Stephen appeared. Kit sucked in a sharp breath, dreading what he might hear.

"Marcus, a word if you please," Stephen said, stepping forward and leveling a hard look at Kit as he did. "I'm afraid Kit's companions gave us the slip," he said.

Kit almost staggered under the relief of those words. He closed his eyes briefly, sending up a swift prayer of thanks as hot tears welled under his eyelids. Alec and Robert were safe; he couldn't imagine that anything in life would ever sound as sweet as that.

"Damn you," Marcus snapped. Kit surreptitiously scrubbed a hand over his eyes, trying desperately to get his trembling limbs under control.

"They're trained City Guardsmen," Stephen said, his tone conciliatory, even as he kept a wary watch on Marcus's face.

"You should have taken care of it yourself," Marcus growled.

"What's done is done," Stephen said. "Do you want us to continue the search?"

Kit held his breath, ready to risk another beating to plead his friends' case one last time.

"I'll not waste any more time here," Marcus said. "Leave some men to continue the hunt, otherwise instruct everybody to pack. We leave as soon as we can." Stephen saluted and strode out.

Marcus turned quickly, and Kit tensed, expecting further violence, but Marcus only regarded him suspiciously. "Why did you come back?" he asked. "You were eager enough to flee from Shrewsbury and run halfway across the country, yet you returned of your own accord. It makes no sense."

Kit decided to risk the truth, at least the part that would not enrage Marcus further. "The Guardsmen would not see me hang simply because of my relationship to you. I would not see them killed for the same reason."

"That's it?" Marcus pressed, his forehead furrowing. "You returned here, knowing what you would face, because you thought to spare two complete strangers?"

"They should not have to pay for their compassion with their lives," Kit said.

Marcus shook his head. "Three years at my side and you've learned nothing," he sneered. He raised a hand, and Kit steeled himself, but Marcus only unclasped a thick gold chain from around his neck.

Kit blanched when he saw it, a mark of ownership that Marcus had forced him to wear, one he had been overjoyed to abandon when Alec had helped him flee.

"You misplaced my gift, I see," Marcus said quietly, though his expression told Kit that he knew well how it had come to end up discarded on the dirt floor of a filthy tavern in Shrewsbury.

Kit nodded mutely.

Marcus arched an eyebrow, and Kit turned, shuddering when the warmed metal settled against his skin. Marcus pulled tight, and the clasp closed through a new loop, so the links bit into his throat. He swallowed painfully, the familiar weight of the collar pressing him down, a fitting reflection of the heaviness of heart that was stealing over him.

"That's much better," Marcus said. He spun Kit around and tapped his chin, forcing him to look up into stormy eyes. "I've put up with a lot from you, Kit," he continued softly. "I've allowed more leniency than I should have. But my patience has worn thin. From here on in, it will be very simple. Prove to me that you are worth the effort, or expect the worst. There will be no more clemency."

The despair that had settled over Kit burrowed deeper, spreading through him, though with it came a surprising calm. He knew that there would be no more escape attempts for him. Even if Marcus hadn't vowed to restrict his movements, the last of the fight had been truly beaten out of him this time. He felt the dull, deep ache of all that was now lost to him; Alec and Robert were gone, his family no longer needed him. He had no more reason to resist.

"Whatever pleases you," he said wearily, his shoulders sagging in defeat.

Time would pass, his looks would fade, and his grace would falter, and Marcus would eventually lose interest. Until that time, he vowed to close his heart to everything but the here and now, to bury the hope and love that had so recently been awakened, to narrow his world once again to Marcus's unrelenting demands and the achingly familiar emptiness that rose up to engulf his soul.

CHAPTER 12

IT HAD been surprisingly easy to find this place, Alec mused, considering the fact that Marcus de Crecy was one of the most sought-after villains in the land. He shifted his weight, massaging the stiffness out of his right knee and wondering at his softness. Time was he could stalk his prey for endless hours, watching in silence for just the right moment to reveal himself. Today he had been hiding amongst the trees on a small rise above a ramshackle inn for barely an hour before his knees had begun to ache at the forced inactivity. He sighed heavily, vowing to return to the daily conditioning routine that Robert had devised to ensure they remained flexible and strong, then smiling wryly at his own optimism. He would have to survive first, before making any such plans.

When he and Robert had stepped out of the alleyway opposite the inn this morning, they had immediately caught sight of the two men who had been following them, one still bleeding profusely from the head, where Robert had slammed him into the wall. They had soon been joined by a man Alec knew was called Stephen, whom he recognized from a previous encounter when Kit was still simply a thief being escorted to Shrewsbury to face justice.

It seemed like a lifetime ago.

It had been simple to pursue the three men as they mounted up and rode north; they certainly hadn't taken any care to cover their tracks, and Alec assumed it was because they didn't expect to be followed. He and Robert had silently shadowed them as they covered the mile or so before stopping at the tavern below and disappearing inside. After a hurried conversation, Alec had settled down to keep watch, while Robert turned his mount back down the track and disappeared up the road to Boston.

Alec waited patiently, turning over the details of their plan, examining the points at which things could go wrong, and finding an alarmingly high number. Though he knew he had to keep a clear head, he couldn't help wondering how Kit fared, and it seemed inevitable that his mind would turn to his own capture and imprisonment by the Sun League some three years earlier. Robert had risked all to rescue him, had found him more dead than alive, and had slowly encouraged him back to the land of the living, despite his surly protestations.

It had been a hard road, dealing with the horror of his torture and humiliation on top of the pain of being parted from Jamie. But Robert had stuck by him, had forced him to face both hurts, and had pushed him relentlessly forward. Alec only hoped that he would be given the same opportunity on Kit's behalf.

Alec's knee had begun to ache in earnest when Stephen suddenly reappeared and began to issue orders, and the courtyard sprang to life as the men who had been idling there started moving with purpose. With a sinking heart, Alec realized that they were preparing to leave. The sun had not yet reached its full height, and Alec guessed it was just past noon, still hours left in the day if the party below intended to travel. He swore under his breath; he couldn't be sure how long it would take Robert to regain Boston and put their plan into action, and if the activity in the courtyard was anything to go by, de Crecy could be long gone before Robert returned.

Sending up a quick prayer, and trying not to contemplate Robert's furious reaction, he caught at the reins of his mount, left his hiding place, and walked slowly down a slippery incline toward the inn. By the time he found himself out from under the cover of the trees and fully exposed, several shadowy figures had detached themselves from various points around the tavern. As he turned onto the path that led to the front of the building, he saw the glint of the sun reflecting from the metal tips of a dozen arrows and off the blades of the bristling swords that suddenly surrounded him.

He held out his hands, palms facing upward to indicate that he was unarmed, and called out, "I'm here to see Marcus de Crecy."

"What business do you have with Marcus?" a voice demanded.

Alec glanced around until he locked eyes with Stephen. "My business is my own," he said calmly. "You may tell him it concerns Kit Porter."

Stephen's eyes widened and his sword remained pointed at Alec's heart, but he nodded and stood aside, and Alec dropped the reins he was holding and stepped across the threshold and into the gloom.

He was escorted into a small room, furnished simply with a few benches and a wooden table, on which sat the remnants of a meal. Stephen looked around briefly, then crossed to the fireplace and bent his head to speak directly into the ear of somebody sitting in one of the great wooden chairs that flanked the grate. The man listened intently, then leaned forward, and Alec found himself looking into the dark eyes of Marcus de Crecy. Though he had only glimpsed the man briefly when de Crecy had tried to kill Kit, that cruel face had been seared in Alec's memory.

"What brings you here?" de Crecy asked.

"I've come about the boy," Alec replied, seeing no reason to dissemble. "I'm here to bargain for his freedom."

He glanced around, but Kit was nowhere to be seen. For a brief moment, he wondered whether he was too late, but the covetous gleam in de Crecy's eyes told him that Marcus still wanted Kit, and whatever else he might be planning, he hadn't dispatched his favorite.

If Marcus was surprised, he didn't show it. His expression remained impassive as his eyes fixed steadily on Alec's face. "You'd have me turn him over to you?" he said, his eyebrows arching. "So you can finish the job and drag him off to the hangman's noose? I know who you are, Captain Weston."

Alec shrugged. "Then you must also know that I am no longer a captain in the City Guard."

"So I've been told. Kit assures me you saved his life," de Crecy said. "Why did you do that? It clearly cost you much."

Alec made a gesture, as though brushing the subject aside. "I would not have the death of an innocent on my hands," he said.

Marcus snorted. "Hardly an innocent," he said dryly. "He's been a member of my household for three years. There's very little he hasn't done for me."

"Against his will," Alec put in.

"I didn't think your masters were concerned with such niceties," Marcus snapped.

Alec bit his tongue, knowing that there was little defense against the accusation. Anthony Arlen, who had sent him on the mission to capture Kit, had tried to use the boy as bait to catch a bigger fish and had cared not a whit that Kit's life had been endangered in the process. Still, Marcus de Crecy had also played Kit false.

"You are scarcely in a position to judge the behavior of others," he retorted. "When you realized you could not rescue the boy, you tried to kill him."

Marcus inclined his head, tacitly acknowledging the observation. "Which brings me back to the question of why you are here. You saved him from Arlen's noose, you protected him from my reprisal. Your conscience should be assuaged. And yet you turn up here making demands."

"I ask only for his freedom," Alec said. "As you say, you have had him for three years. He deserves a chance at an honest life."

"And what do you offer to secure his liberty?" Marcus asked.

Alec tried to hide his surprise, wondering if it could possibly be as easy as this. "I have money," he said, swiftly calculating how much his house would fetch and whether he could appeal to Jamie for a loan.

Marcus's lips curled into a sneer. "I doubt you could raise enough," he said. "I would find his special talents hard to replace."

"What would it take to free him?" Alec demanded, revolted by de Crecy's leering manner and unwilling to continue this game. "I will do anything."

A light flared in de Crecy's eyes, and then they narrowed speculatively. "Anything?" he echoed. "He must mean a great deal to you." He made a quick series of hand gestures, which Alec recognized as the secret language of the Sun League, and Stephen hurried out of the room.

"Sit," Marcus said, waving a hand to indicate the seat opposite him. "I'm sure we can come to some agreement."

Alec approached cautiously and sat in the chair opposite Marcus, sinking into its soft cushions and protected from the fire's heat by the wings that protruded from the high back. He shot surreptitious glances at de Crecy, trying to gauge what he could. Though his skin was faintly pockmarked and bore several ugly scars, there was something undeniably compelling about his imposing figure. His eyes seemed unnaturally dark, and his long hair, gathered into a tight braid that hung halfway down his back, was black as a raven's wing and shone in the firelight. Though still and silent, he gave off an unmistakable air of menace, and Alec shivered at the thought of Kit at this man's mercy.

Marcus was watching him with equal intensity, though his expression was so guarded that Alec had no idea what was going through his mind. Marcus looked up and smiled when the door behind Alec opened. He beckoned and a figure walked past Alec's chair and bent awkwardly to brush a kiss against Marcus's upturned cheek. "You wanted to see me, Marcus?" Kit said, his back toward Alec as he straightened.

Alec's breath caught in his throat. It was clear from Kit's stiff gait and from the dried blood streaking his loose cotton shirt that he had been mistreated. Alec bit down on his lip to stop himself from saying something he would surely later regret, though anger boiled in him.

"We have a visitor, Kit," Marcus said genially, gesturing toward Alec.

Kit turned, his eyes widening in shock when he saw Alec, and all the color drained from his face.

"Alec, what are you doing here?" he gasped, his voice filled with dismay.

His cheek was scraped raw, and there was a fresh cut on the back of his hand. Alec stared at Kit's bleak, hopeless expression, and suddenly all thought of stalling went out of his head.

"My life in exchange for his," he blurted, dropping any pretense at detachment. "Do what you want with me, but let the boy go free."

"Alec, no," Kit gasped, looking horrified. He stepped forward, but Marcus grabbed his wrist and tugged him sharply backward.

Alec shot to his feet, freezing when a sword appeared out of nowhere, scraping his throat so closely that he knew it had drawn blood. Out of the corner of his eye, he saw Stephen, arm unwavering as he held Alec at bay, and around him several other men had unsheathed their weapons in a sinister whisper of steel, all ready to run him through at the merest gesture from de Crecy.

Marcus was holding Kit fast, his eyes glittering with barely contained rage. "Thank you, Captain Weston," he hissed. "You've just answered a burning question." He nodded toward Stephen. "Take him away," he ordered. "I need a few moments with Kit."

KIT watched helplessly as Alec was dragged out of the room, his mind reeling with questions, though all thoughts vanished when Marcus spun him around and slammed him up against the wall beside the fireplace. Kit gasped as the stripes on his back reopened and a warm trickle of blood slid down between his shoulder blades.

Marcus grabbed his chin, forcing his head up. "I knew it!" he spat. "It's the only explanation that made any sense." His hand tightened painfully. "He's had you."

"Marcus, I—"

"Don't deny it," Marcus growled, slamming Kit's head back against the wall. "Why else would he risk everything for you? Tell me, did he force you?"

"No!" Kit choked out.

"You gave yourself freely?" Marcus hissed. "How dare you give to him what belongs to me." He let go suddenly, and Kit slumped against the wall, pain shooting across his back. "I will kill him for this," Marcus said coldly.

Kit flinched. "Do what you want with me, but Alec is blameless."

"You are both so eager to sacrifice yourself for the other," Marcus sneered. "It is quite touching."

"Marcus, please," Kit begged. "I will do whatever you want...."

Marcus whirled around again and once more pinned Kit against the wall. The brickwork dug into him, scraping his lacerated skin. Marcus reached a hand and dragged it through Kit's hair, the caress as violent as a blow. "What makes you think you have anything I still want?" he hissed.

Kit's blood ran cold at the look of contempt that flared on Marcus's face. His gaze flickered to the doorway as Stephen walked back into the room, but he knew there would be no help there. Marcus pressed closer, his face only inches from Kit's own. "Since you are so willing to share your body with this man, you can also share his fate."

Marcus stepped back, breathing hard, and snapped his fingers in Stephen's direction. "Get him out of my sight," he shouted. "Let him join the Guardsman. They will no doubt want to say their farewells before I gut them both."

Too dazed to think of resisting, Kit allowed Stephen to escort him out of the chamber and into the courtyard.

"Why did you have to tell him that, Kit?" Stephen asked. "You can't save the captain, but you could have saved yourself. I'd not have spoken about what was between you."

"You knew?" Kit gasped.

Stephen shrugged. "I guessed it easily enough. If I had not already seen it in your eyes, I certainly saw it in his."

"Can you intercede for us, Stephen?" Kit asked quietly. "Marcus might listen to you."

Stephen shook his head ruefully. "I'll do whatever I can for you," he said. "But I'm afraid there will be no mercy for the Guardsman."

"And Robert, his friend?" Kit asked. "Did you capture him alongside Alec?" He stopped as they reached a small storage shed, guarded by two armed men, without doubt the place in which Alec was imprisoned.

"I did not capture the captain," Stephen said, frowning. "He walked in and surrendered himself."

"God, what has he done?" Kit whispered.

Stephen signaled and one of the guards opened the door. "I'll plead your case, Kit. But I cannot promise he'll be moved."

"Thank you, my friend," Kit replied. He crossed the threshold, spotting Alec sitting in a corner atop a sack of grain, before the door closed behind him, and the room was plunged into darkness.

As his eyes grew accustomed to the gloom, he became aware that Alec had moved and was standing right in front of him. A moment later, a cool hand cupped his cheek.

"Kit, I'm so sorry," Alec said softly. "I did not mean for this to happen."

Kit covered the fingers with his own. "You should not have come," he said desperately. "You should be miles away by now."

"I'd not leave you in that man's hands," Alec said.

"It would have been fine," Kit insisted.

"He has already hurt you," Alec said, his fingers ghosting over Kit's torn cheek.

"I thought you and Robert were safe. That made it easy to bear his temper," Kit replied. "But now…. He means to kill you, Alec."

Alec dismissed his words with a gesture. "And what of you?" he asked urgently.

Kit tried to look away, but Alec held him fast. "Stephen will speak on my behalf," he said slowly.

"And if he fails?" Alec pressed.

Kit shrugged. "Then I am to share your fate."

"God's wounds," Alec hissed. He clutched Kit's shoulders. "I did not think to put you in danger," he said. "I thought all for the best." He tugged gently, and Kit stepped into the shelter of his arms. "I'd never have left you this morning if I'd known the League was so close," Alec whispered against his ear. He clutched Kit tightly for a moment, then abruptly pushed him to arm's length.

"Promise me you will do whatever is necessary to survive," he said urgently.

"I'll not abandon you—" Kit started, flinching when Alec tightened his fingers.

"Agree to whatever de Crecy demands of you," Alec interrupted harshly. "Regardless of his threats against me."

Kit shrugged Alec's hands off him. "You cannot ask of me what you would not do yourself," he said stubbornly.

"You must buy yourself some time," Alec pleaded. He shook his head as though in frustration. "God, I cannot believe I have brought you to this. If I had only listened to Robert!"

"Where is Robert?" Kit asked. "Tell me at least that he is spared all this."

Alec opened his mouth, but his reply was swallowed up as the door once again creaked on its rusty hinges and Stephen appeared in the doorway. "Marcus wants to see you," he said, beckoning them out.

They crossed the courtyard quickly, their progress followed by a dozen curious pairs of eyes. Kit glanced sidelong at Stephen, but the man only shook his head. Kit's heart sank as they were escorted back into the hall to find Marcus watching them through hooded eyes, his men silently ringing him with swords drawn.

"I take it your reunion was tender?" Marcus scoffed.

"Why are you doing this?" Alec asked, the simplicity of the question seeming to catch Marcus off guard. "Kit did not betray the League," Alec continued, addressing the gathered men as much as their leader. "Despite the threats and promises, he remained true."

"Which is why he isn't already dead," Marcus said coldly. "You, on the other hand, will not find me so forgiving. You took something that belonged to me. There's a price to be paid for that."

"I will gladly pay your price," Alec said. "But let the boy go. He doesn't deserve to die for running from the man who would have killed him."

"Silence!" Marcus roared, as a murmur rippled through his men. The room stilled again as Stephen took a step forward.

"He's right, Marcus," Stephen said calmly. "Kit didn't betray us, though he was sorely pressed. Punish him for disobedience, cast him out of your favor if you must, but abide by the justice of the League."

A wave of muttering once again rose and swelled, some voices louder than the rest, and much to Kit's surprise, all in support of sparing his life. Though he knew that the majority of those present cared little for him, he was heartened that Stephen's appeal to their peculiar code of fairness held some sway.

Marcus looked around at the swords now wavering in the hands of his men, then barked out a command, and silence fell once more. He turned his head back toward Kit, studying him thoughtfully.

"I would grant you your life," he said slowly. "I would even take you back into my household. But I want to hear you ask for my pardon and you'll have to accept any punishment I see fit."

Kit heard Alec breathe out a sigh of relief, and out of the corner of his eye, he saw a triumphant grin light up Stephen's face. But he knew Marcus well enough to realize that the man had not yet finished. "But as you know," Marcus added loudly, confirming Kit's suspicions, "my forgiveness comes at a price. The Guardsman's life is forfeit."

Though not unexpected, Kit nevertheless felt his heart knot in despair. He risked a glance at Alec, whose whole expression urged him to accept the terms. Stephen was nodding encouragement, and even Marcus's men were easy enough to read as they wordlessly counseled reason.

Kit turned back and looked into Marcus's cold eyes. It was clear that he thought the outcome assured, and that he meant this to be a lesson Kit would not soon forget. Kit took a step closer, bowing his head before sinking slowly to his knees, aware of every eye on him.

"I beg your pardon and ask for mercy," he said contritely. Marcus leaned forward in his chair, and Kit raised his head. "Not for myself but for Captain Weston," he said, his voice echoing in the silent hall.

Marcus roared an oath and leapt to his feet, his fist clenched. But as he bore down on Kit, a loud commotion erupted from outside the door. Kit looked around in confusion and caught Alec's eye, then scrambled to his feet as Alec gestured with his head to indicate that Kit should get out of the way. He backed up quickly, gaining Alec's side as several swords were leveled in their direction.

"Watch them," Marcus shouted, and began to stride to the door.

He had barely taken three steps when the door burst open, and several uniformed City Guardsmen rushed in with swords drawn, led by Robert, focused and determined and lit with righteous anger.

"Robert, to me!" Alec shouted. Robert tossed a sword up into the air, its handle falling uncannily into Alec's outstretched hand, and a moment later, he was standing beside Alec, his own sword in his right hand, and a short-handled dagger in his left.

"What kept you?" Alec grinned.

"You were not where you were supposed to be," Robert barked. "When this is over, you and I will be having words." Any further admonishments were swallowed up when Marcus's men surged toward them.

Kit looked around desperately, and when Robert dispatched one of his opponents with two swift strikes, Kit picked up the fallen man's sword and went to stand next to his friends.

"Good to see you, boy," Robert said, breathing hard.

Kit didn't have time to return the greeting, although he felt it with all his heart. He looked around quickly and saw that Marcus and Stephen were both being hard pressed by the Guard, but he didn't have time to consider their situation before Marcus's men once again surged forward. Unable to spare a thought for anybody else, he steadied his sword arm and closed in on his attackers.

The ring of steel on steel filled the air, coupled with shouts and oaths, and the astonished gasps of wounded men who could not quite believe they were fated to die here. Kit's arm ached with the parry and thrust of defense and attack, though he felt no joy in dealing blows, even to those who had openly despised and tormented him.

When he found a moment to look about him, he saw that Marcus had fought his way through several Guardsmen and was now face to face with Alec. They circled each other, testing for weakness, both with a fierce look of concentration on their faces. Kit flinched as Marcus lunged at Alec's head, and only breathed again when Alec neatly parried the move and slashed at Marcus's right side. The stroke caught Marcus's cloak, though mercifully the sword did not get tangled, only sliced a ragged hunk of it off.

The two men were evenly matched for speed and skill, though Kit had good cause to know that Marcus had some tricks up his sleeve that he doubted Alec had learned from his fencing master. So when Marcus tried something underhanded, Kit was surprised to see how easily Alec dodged the move—until he glanced over at Robert's satisfied smirk and it became apparent these two had engaged in private lessons not offered by the City Guard.

After that, the rules of engagement were swiftly abandoned, and they scrapped and brawled like the lowest street rogues, until Marcus attempted a vicious thrust with his dagger that unbalanced him. Clutching at Alec's tunic, the two of them fell to the floor in a mass of limbs and blades, and when the dust settled, Alec's sword was resting across Marcus's naked throat, barely biting into the flesh. Marcus sucked in a breath and stilled, his dagger clattering to the ground as he released his hold and silently surrendered.

Kit had never seen Marcus give in so easily, so when Alec relaxed his hold and started to rise to his feet, Kit kept his eyes locked on Marcus's face. It was only long familiarity with the man's many moods that allowed him to recognize the tiny change in Marcus's expression that betrayed his intent.

"Alec!" Kit yelled.

He threw himself onto his knees, his knife slashing downward as Marcus twisted suddenly to grab for his discarded dagger. Kit felt his knife connect, tearing through soft flesh as he pinned Marcus's hand to the dirt floor.

Marcus turned his head sharply, and Kit recoiled as their eyes met and Marcus grimaced in agony, though he made no sound. For one fleeting moment, Kit felt an absurd urge to beg forgiveness; then he was pushed aside roughly as Robert crowded in behind him.

Kit flinched when Robert yanked the blade out of Marcus's hand. Blood dripped down Marcus's doublet as one of the Guards hauled him roughly to his feet and began to tie his hands behind his back. Marcus gazed down at Kit, still kneeling at his feet, and his lips curled into a scornful sneer.

"It seems as though you learned something from me after all," he said.

Kit felt frozen to the spot, unable to break free. He swallowed hard, struggling to reconcile the feelings that churned in him. Marcus and the Sun League had shaped so much of his life, had forged him through hardship and torment. He wondered if he knew anymore how to make a life without them, if he knew who he was without Marcus de Crecy to define him.

"Kit." Alec's urgent voice broke the spell, and he turned his head and looked into kinder eyes. "Are you all right?" Alec asked, his voice softening.

Kit nodded as he struggled to his feet and looked around, relieved to see that Robert and Alec were whole, though both were bleeding from small wounds. With an odd sense of relief, he saw that Stephen had also been spared, and with him several of Marcus's followers, and most of the City Guard appeared unharmed, despite the amount of blood soaking into the rush matting underfoot.

"Captain Weston," Marcus said, his voice pulling Kit's gaze back to him. "You will take care of my boy, won't you? As soon as I deal with this little mess, I'm coming back for him."

Kit shuddered, and a moment later he felt Alec's hand, warm against the back of his neck. With a quick twist, Alec unclasped the gold chain that Marcus had locked around Kit's throat and dropped it into the dirt at Marcus's feet. Kit felt a surge of relief course through him, despite his fear.

"I think this little mess might keep you occupied for a good while," Alec replied coolly. "And I doubt anybody will be seeing much of you once the Lord Chancellor has extended his hospitality."

Marcus laughed, sounding genuinely unconcerned. "It's a long way to London," he said. "And we have many friends willing to help us, Captain. That's something you should know firsthand."

Alec frowned. "Your meaning?" he asked.

"How do you think we knew to come to Boston?" Marcus replied.

"You tracked us—"

"We were told," Marcus cut in. "As we were told the last time you fell into the Sun League's hands."

"Who told you?" Robert demanded, coming to stand beside Kit.

Marcus shook his head. "It doesn't pay to betray my sources," he said. "But if I were you, I'd reconsider those you think of as friends."

The Guardsman tugged at Marcus's bonds, and he took a step back. His eyes swiveled back to Kit as he said, "I'll be seeing you soon, boy," before being hustled out of the room along with his men. Stephen gave a final nod in Kit's direction, and Kit managed a weak smile, acknowledging the cautious friendship that Stephen had offered, albeit tempered by his allegiance to Marcus.

"What do you think de Crecy meant?" Robert asked, but Kit could only shrug, unwilling to consider too closely the awful implication of betrayal.

They made their way out of the inn and into the courtyard, where Marcus and his men were already mounted and being led away. One of the Guardsmen crossed to them, stopped in front of Alec, and saluted crisply. "We are indebted to you, Captain Weston," he said. "As you are aware, the Lord Chancellor has been keen to secure the arrest of this gang, but found it difficult in their home county, where they are protected by the populace."

"It will be no easy feat to find any evidence against them," Alec warned.

"We will do what we can," the Guardsman said. "Will you accompany us back to Boston? The Lord Chancellor has been sent for. I'm sure he will want to thank you in person."

"We have our own duties to attend to," Robert said quickly.

"As you wish." The Guardsman saluted again and mounted his horse, then trotted out of the courtyard after his men.

"What was that about?" Alec murmured as soon as the Guard was out of earshot. "I thought we'd be tied up and hauled off alongside de Crecy."

"I didn't exactly tell the truth when I asked for his help," Robert replied, saluting as the Guard rode off. "I told them we'd been playing decoy in order to lure de Crecy off his home turf. I told them we worked on Arlen's explicit instructions and that he'd have their heads if they let the Lord Chancellor's most wanted criminal slip through their fingers."

Alec laughed. "It won't take long for that story to unravel when Arlen gets here."

"Which is why I suggest we're not here when he arrives," Robert said. He turned toward Kit. "I'm sorry if this will cause problems for your family. Believe me, there was no other way."

Kit nodded. "The League will not hold me responsible. I did not betray them," he said. "As for my mother...." He swallowed hard and his voice trembled slightly when he continued. "She made her choice. She is under Marcus's protection now." He glanced between Robert and Alec. "Thank you both," he said. "You once again risked your lives for me."

"Let's not make it a habit," Robert said dryly. "We should get out of here as swiftly as possible."

"Agreed," Alec said.

"And I intend to have words with you both about this bloody shambles," Robert said sternly, though his eyes held a glimmer of mirth.

"Yes, Robert," Alec said contritely, winking at Kit when Robert turned his back.

THEY took the precaution of moving to another inn, this one closer to the dock and filled with travelers too intent on their own business to cast more than a passing look their way. Still, Robert scoured the area carefully until he was satisfied that there were no City Guards or League members nearby. They had decided to stay together this time, so all three of them were crammed into a tiny room behind the kitchen, with the heat and smell of roasting meat and fresh baked bread seeping through the thin walls.

Robert and Alec were perched on the single narrow cot, with Kit sitting on the floor, all in shirtsleeves against the oppressive warmth.

"Who do you think told de Crecy where to find us?" Robert asked.

Alec shifted uncomfortably and shook his head.

"Could it not have been somebody we met on the journey?" Kit asked, and Alec could tell that he didn't want to face the possibility that somebody close had betrayed them.

"De Crecy said it was a friend," Alec mused.

"Surely just to anger you," Robert said. His gaze swiveled to Kit's face. "Is that possible?"

Alec watched as Kit's brow furrowed. "It isn't really like him," he said reluctantly, glancing quickly into Alec's eyes. "I've never known him to lie. He's never had to," he continued. "People do his bidding out of fear. He has never needed any other tactic."

Little as Alec wanted to consider other possibilities, he nodded in agreement. "It didn't sound like an idle boast," he said. "I think we have to assume that somebody close gave us up. And if de Crecy is to be believed, it was the same person who betrayed me to the Sun League three years ago."

Robert looked distinctly uncomfortable. "There were very few who knew our destination," he pointed out.

"And Jamie is beyond reproach," Alec said firmly.

Robert's features hardened. "Then we only have one other choice."

Alec looked away, his gut tightening, his throat closing over the words.

"Mrs. McEwen," Kit whispered, sparing Alec the need to give voice to the hated name. Alec shook his head mutely, unwilling to believe it of her.

"She knew Jamie was helping us," Kit said softly, his troubled eyes darting to Alec's face.

"And it would take little wit to discover which ships were sailing and from where," Robert added.

"But why?" Alec murmured, unable to comprehend the depth of hate needed to betray him so viciously.

Robert fetched up a deep sigh. "Did you ever ask yourself how I knew you were… different to other men?" he asked softly.

Alec started, surprised that Robert would want to discuss that now. They had never spoken about it, even though Alec had realized a long time ago that Robert knew things about him that he'd kept hidden from the rest of the world.

"She told me," Robert said. "Mrs. Alexander James McEwen."

Alec felt a cold sweat break out over his body, then felt his skin flush with fevered heat. He couldn't get his lips to form any words, though his head overflowed with questions.

"It was just after you'd joined the Guard," Robert said. "I was called into the commander's office. I didn't know who she was, although it was clear she was quality. She told me things about you. She made accusations…."

He trailed off, but when the silence stretched on, Alec still unable to give voice to his shock, Robert picked up the story again. "I told her in no uncertain terms that you were proving yourself to be a good and loyal member of the Guard, and that as long as I didn't hear any complaints against you, I'd judge you as you presented yourself and not on gossip, regardless of its source. She didn't take that too well," he said sardonically. "For obvious reasons, she wouldn't identify herself, but the commander let it slip that she was Alexander McEwen's wife."

"She tried to ruin me?" Alec whispered. "But why? I'd already left the house. I barely saw Jamie anymore."

"Because she'd lied to you both and she was afraid," Robert said. "She wanted you as far away from Ludlow as possible. She didn't want to run the risk that you and Jamie would start speaking again and expose her deceit."

Kit shifted restlessly. "It explains what happened when the League captured you," he said softly. "You were of little value to them. And if they'd wanted you dead, they would have killed you outright. They had to be acting under contract."

"They wanted to break you," Robert said harshly. "She must have paid handsomely to ensure that you were in no condition to renew your friendship with Jamie."

The heat began to recede from Alec's body, leaving him clearheaded and lucid. It made a twisted kind of sense. He had certainly found it impossible in the following years to contemplate Ludlow without gut-wrenching horror.

"So you think she's the informant?" he asked. "You think she sold us to the Guard, and when that failed, she betrayed us to the League?"

"Who else?" Robert replied. "She certainly hates you enough, she made that clear."

An image of her face rose in Alec's mind, twisted beyond recognition by contempt and loathing. He remembered her condemnation of her own son, her declaration that she'd rather see him dead than continuing to sin against nature. Certainly she was cunning enough to trick Jamie into sharing what he knew about their travel plans, and it would be easy to determine their most likely destination based on the meticulous accounts Jamie kept in his shipping ledger.

Robert obviously read the moment when Alec accepted the chilling truth. "What do you want to do about it?" he asked.

Alec shrugged. "What would you have me do? I have no proof."

"She put all our lives in danger, and you'd let her get away with it?" Robert blazed.

"I'll not accuse her in front of Jamie," Alec replied stonily. "She would deny it, and it would only sow discord between us."

"I can't believe you continue to protect her!"

"I do it to protect Jamie," Alec said, his voice rising angrily.

"Did you ever consider it in his best interests to know what a treacherous bitch she really is?" Robert retorted.

"We are at least safe," Kit said quickly, attempting to diffuse the tension. "Whatever she may have planned for us was averted."

Alec pulled in a deep breath, fighting for control. "Kit is right," he said, his eyes silently appealing to Robert to drop the subject. He knew that on dark, sleepless nights, he would be haunted by the evidence of her bitter hatred and would have to eventually give voice to his grief, but right now it felt too raw.

Robert's eyes locked with his, and Alec watched in relief as the dark anger slowly receded. "What now, then?" Robert asked gruffly. "Arlen has de Crecy, so he might be persuaded to call the City Guard off our trail, but I don't doubt he'll still see Kit as the key to finishing de Crecy off."

"And without Marcus's protection, I'm not sure how I'll be regarded by the League," Kit said softly. "I don't think they've ever let anybody escape them before."

"So we're back where we started," Alec said morosely.

Silence settled in on them until Robert cleared his throat noisily.

"If nothing has changed, why don't we stick with our plan?" he suggested. "There's little enough to keep us in England, and a few months away might resolve some of our problems, or at least show them in a truer light."

The three of them exchanged looks, none venturing an opinion until a smile transformed Kit's face. "Why not?" he asked tentatively. "We'll be away long enough for most of this to be forgotten. We'll be out of the reach of the Guard and the League."

Two pairs of expectant eyes fixed on Alec's face. He looked from one to the other: Robert, whose loyalty and fierce support had always made so much possible; Kit, whose deepening love and commitment enriched his life beyond measure. He couldn't imagine forging a future without either by his side.

A smile twitched at Robert's lips, and Alec knew that once again his decision had been read before he was even aware he'd made it.

"The *Alexander McEwen* sails at daybreak," he said. "I think Captain Grey will find three new recruits on board."

AN OVERNIGHT rainfall had washed the world clean and left a wet sparkle on the cobbled streets below as Kit leaned over the ship's railing and watched the port of Boston bustle into life. Though still early in the morning, the quay teemed with activity as newly arrived vessels were unloaded of their goods and departing boats were packed with all manner of merchandise bound for foreign parts. The hold of the *Alexander McEwen* was being methodically filled with bales of wool and great wooden kegs of salt, all carried on under the watchful eye of a customs official who noted each in a leather-bound ledger.

"Not long now."

Alec's voice sounded close in Kit's ear, and he turned to smile at his friend, who came up alongside him and leaned against the railing. He nodded toward Captain Grey, who was engaged in a heated conversation with the customs agent. "He's just supervising the final tally, then we'll be setting sail."

"It doesn't look as though they agree," Kit murmured.

Alec laughed. "They rarely do," he said wryly. "It's a question of money. The wool is taxed by the King, who must have the lion's share. Jamie tells me his profit margin is so slim that even a single bale miscounted can make a difference."

They watched in silence as the argument continued, Kit wondering whether the two would ever agree so they could get underway. He glanced sideways at Alec, deeply stirred by his handsome features. Robert had given them an hour alone the previous night, trying to hide a smirk as he set out after supper, loudly proclaiming that he would be gone for a while. Kit had winced at his obvious ploy, but Alec had simply laughed and wasted no time in stripping Kit down to his cotton shirt, before stopping suddenly as Kit's fresh hurts were revealed for the first time.

"God's wounds, what did that bastard do to you?" Alec breathed.

He ghosted a hand over Kit's body, barely touching, until Kit grabbed his hand and drew it close.

"He's gone," Kit said, though a flicker of fear managed to break the surface of his joy.

"Aye," Alec agreed. "And you know all that talk of reclaiming you was mere bluster? Arlen will hold him fast, I promise."

Kit nodded, although he did not feel nearly as certain as Alec. Marcus had never been thwarted before, though plenty had tried.

Alec gently tipped his chin up until Kit was looking into deep blue eyes. "I promise," Alec repeated, more firmly this time so that Kit could almost believe him.

Alec tugged him close, and Kit breathed the comforting scents of carbolic soap, leather, and the faint smell of clean sweat. Though Alec refused to follow when Kit nodded toward the bed, voicing concern over Kit's hurts, his callused hand had closed around Kit's stiffening prick and he had offered sweet release along with breathless kisses, his careful ministrations making Kit shudder and moan and yearn for more.

When they had finished, Alec drew him down gently onto the mattress and wrapped strong arms around him, whispering of the wonders that lay ahead until he fell into blissful sleep.

Kit was dragged back to the present when Robert appeared suddenly on his left side and muttered, "No doubt the right bribe was finally tendered."

Refocusing on the quayside, Kit breathed a sigh of relief to see that Captain Grey and the custom's official had stopped gesticulating and were now shaking hands cordially.

Captain Grey finally stalked up the gangplank, shouting last instructions, and moments after he had gained the deck, ropes were untied, sails unfurled, and the ship slipped its moorings and drifted to the middle of the river. It turned in a slow half circle until facing south, then rode the lapping currents, navigating easily past small vessels and great barges alike.

They followed the banks of the river, watching silently as warehouses and storage barns receded into the distance, giving way to leafy woodland, vast green fields, and flat marshlands, until they rounded a final long bend and gained the mouth of the Witham as it widened into the estuary of the Wash.

Kit felt the ship sway and roll under his feet as she turned east into the great square bay, her canvas sails filling quickly with the blowing breeze. The sailors on board were more active now, running from bow to stern as they loosened ropes and trimmed the sails under the watchful eye of Captain Grey. The waters appeared darker here, and the ship rose and fell more noticeably on the swelling tide.

"Take a good look," Alec said. "We'll likely not see these shores again for many months."

Kit turned his head, fixing his eyes on the increasingly distant coast that was slowly slipping from view.

"Any regrets?" Alec asked.

Kit turned to find Alec and Robert watching him keenly. He knew that Alec had asked the question genuinely, expecting a considered response. He let his mind roam, remembering the simple life he had lived before Marcus appeared, his three terrible years at the hands of the Sun League, and the elation that freedom had wrought. He thought of the people who had shaped his life, some taken from him by force, some choosing a destiny that no longer included him. There was undeniable sorrow in the memories, but also a measure of acceptance and peace.

A cool, salt breeze blew against his face, making his skin tingle. Robert and Alec were a solid presence on either side of him, one an increasingly trusted friend, the other a tender lover. Though Kit did not know how he would feel when his homeland was far behind him, and all those he had loved or learned to endure no longer figured in his life, he was certain that this was right.

"No regrets," he said finally.

Robert grinned and held out his hand, and all three of them clasped tightly. "To whatever fate has in store for us," he said.

"To the future," Kit added, and for the first time in his life, he allowed himself to consider the possibility of happiness.

Also from MAGGIE LEE

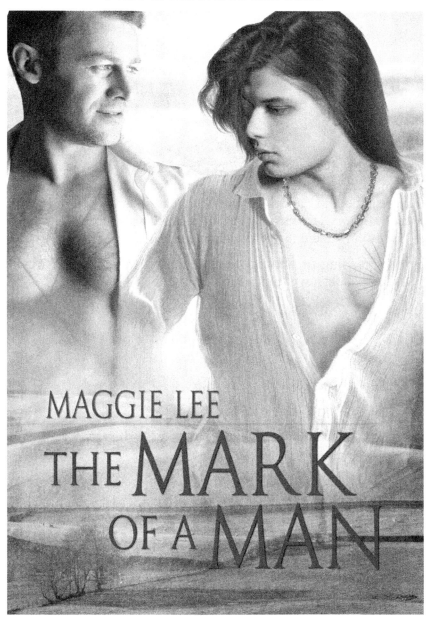

MAGGIE LEE
THE MARK
OF A MAN

http://www.dreamspinnerpress.com

MAGGIE LEE discovered historical fiction when she was in her teens and soon after stumbled across the world of M/M romance; she now takes great delight in combining both passions in her writing. Her interest in history is wide-ranging, from medieval Europe to America's Old West to the ancient worlds of the earliest civilizations.

When not reading or writing, Maggie enjoys traveling and watching movies, and she's never met a musical she didn't like!

Read more by MAGGIE LEE in

http://www.dreamspinnerpress.com

Read more by MAGGIE LEE in

A Dreamspinner Press Anthology

RIDING
DOUBLE

http://www.dreamspinnerpress.com

Romance from DREAMSPINNER PRESS

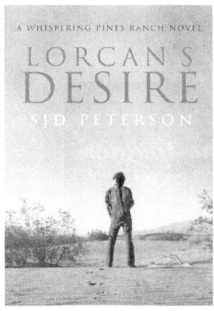

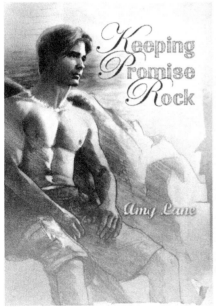

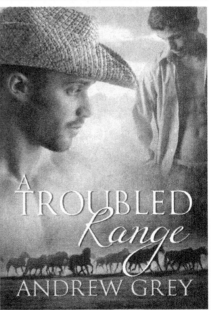

http://www.dreamspinnerpress.com

CPSIA information can be obtained
at www.ICGtesting.com
Printed in the USA
BVOW08s2120261216

471867BV00007B/76/P

9 781623 802509